Emma Tennant was born in London
but spent her childhood in Scotland.
She now lives in West London.

EMMA TENNANT

Two Women of London

The Strange Case of
Ms Jekyll and Mrs Hyde

faber and faber
LONDON · BOSTON

First published in 1989
by Faber and Faber Limited
3 Queen Square London WC1N 3AU
This paperback edition first published in 1990

Photoset by Parker Typesetting Service Leicester
Printed in Great Britain by
Cox & Wyman Ltd, Reading

Emma Tennant is hereby identified as author of this
work in accordance with Section 77 of the Copyright,
Designs and Patents Act 1988.

A CIP record for this book
is available from the British Library

ISBN 0–571–14330–X

For Karl Miller

A man lies dead in the gardens of Rudyard and Nightingale Crescents.

The gravel path, which was raked only this morning by residents and members of the garden committee, is disarranged at the point where it curves round to run alongside Ladbroke Grove, to the east: the hair of the dead man, brown-grey and thin, lies across it like a weed.

As night grows deeper and the noise band of the City drops, leaving a pink glow in a sky that seems permanently overheated, lamps go off in houses either side of the gardens. Chandeliers snap out, like dead stars. In apartments and private dwellings, frosted glass dims softly, children in nurseries turn in their cots and look out through freshly painted bars at the moon.

Below the moon and shining just as bright, the naked light-bulb in Mrs Hyde's kitchen stays on until all hours. It sends a white blade of light over the body of the dead man – and comes into the bedrooms of the Crescents' children, so that they reach out to pull their curtains closer together.

In the morning, the residents will decide to complain about Mrs Hyde's light, in the tatterdemalion house that shouldn't be part of the gardens at all, butting as it does the thronging, littered thoroughfare of Ladbroke Grove.

But by the time they have grumbled to each other on the telephone Roger the gardener will have seen the corpse. Skirting the new saplings, in crinolines of wire netting to protect them from Mrs Hyde's children – and others on the 'wrong end' of one of Notting Hill's most desirable quarters – he will run through Nightingale Passage and bang on Ms Eliza Jekyll's door in the Crescent. Ms Jekyll is kindness itself, and always up early to work on her accounts: Roger has used her telephone before, when his wife was at the hospital.

Today no one comes to the door. As it is mid-February – 8 a.m. on the twelfth, to be exact – the only sign of daylight is the fading of the bar of filmy red across the sky and its replacement by an all-pervading, mottled grey.

Roger rings the bell twice and when he gets no answer he crosses Nightingale Crescent and starts to make his way up Ladbroke Grove, past the vandalized callbox, to the police station. An owl hoots in the gardens as he goes.

The brokers and interior decorators and solicitors and architects who live in these Crescents frown as they reverse their cars from off-street parking areas and set off for work. The cry of the owl, feared by their wives – feared by young, single women who live in basements of elegant mansions – feared by old women in unheated rooms – is no sweet, rural dream here. It is the cry of the prowler, as he makes his way through trees and shrubs to his next victim. Today, under clouds that are like bruises on the dirty, tender pink of a London sky, he will strike again.

Roger the gardener, however, knows better. Going slowly on legs bent from years mowing the lawns of the gardens – and leaving swathes as neat and straight as the

2

lines in a bank book, deposits of grass regularly spaced –
he reaches the top of the Grove and begins to make his
way down the other side. The crenellations of Notting Hill
Police Station come into sight. Roger will report the murder
of a man in the Rudyard/Nightingale Crescent gardens.

All day excitement will spread. From the police themselves, who have spent so long trying to track this man
down. From the press, who will interview past victims;
from TV which takes the victims and sits them blindfold
in the studio to make them talk of rape and violence. And
in all the streets and crescents of the neighbourhood
excitement makes women throw open doors into back
gardens and stretch up to unsnib windows locked for so
long against possible invasion that they give grudgingly
when tried.

Everyone knows the dead man is the Notting Hill
prowler. It is strange that this as-yet unidentified man –
in track shoes, jeans and a battered sports jacket – is more
intimately known than any neighbour or acquaintance.
Nobody knew his face; and yet, as the police vans arrive
and the TV cameras beam their hot, white light in the
February darkness, those who run out and catch a
glimpse of him as he lies there on the path seem to feel
they have lived closely with him for years. And, mixed
with uneasy jubilation, is a sense of loss. The man had
inspired fear; and to some there is a sudden vacuum now
it has gone.

Yet no one fears for Mrs Hyde, who killed the man and
must answer for the crime.

* * *

3

When I was asked by the Executors of the late Dr Frances Crane to try and come up with some kind of an explanation for her sudden illness and death in the summer of 1988 – her peers in the medical profession seeming all equally baffled by the rapid demise of a GP both happy and successful in her career and showing no signs of incipient mental instability – I can say in all truthfulness that if I had had an idea of the frustration (and sheer horror) of the task, I would not have taken it on.

We are surrounded daily by evidence of violence, poverty and misery in this city. The media leave us in no doubt that rapaciousness and a 'loadsamoney' economy have come to represent the highest values in the land. Crime and unrest are on the increase – as, so it seems, are fear and insecurity, which go hand in hand with great wealth and its companion, deprivation.

For all this – and the sad and shocking stories which arise from a society in thrall to greed are many – I would find it hard to believe in the existence of an example stranger or more alarming than the case of Ms Jekyll and Mrs Hyde. And I would go so far as to say that it was by delving too deep into the facts of this distressing episode that Dr Frances Crane met her death. Not physically – no, the cause of her death was coronary thrombosis – but (unproven though it must remain) psychologically: it was as if, on the last occasion before her hospitalization and collapse, she was unable herself to believe what she had discovered and was still, as she admitted, 'in two minds about the possibility of the whole thing'. Her heart gave out, I think, under the strain of trying to reconcile opposites; and, just as we have been told that the holistic approach to medicine may well be our only hope of survival on this earth, so we may find ourselves to blame when it comes to the treatment – manifestly unsuccessful – of the late doctor. No one understood the mental agony she suffered in her last weeks.

Perhaps I am beginning to understand that torment now. I will complete the task of attempting to reconstruct the terrible history of that summer in West London, the summer of '88. Where possible – and for reasons of speed and economy – I have 'described' events – see above – as a writer (presumably) would. Otherwise, in the many significant areas which were, as my friend Robina Sandel of Nightingale Crescent, put it, 'a closed book' to me, I have borrowed extensively from the journals, taped interviews and even, in one case, video film of witnesses and participants in the crime and its consequences.

I think it right, also, to give a list of the 'cast' of this perverse drama. These people have made their names available from a sense of public duty, and in the strong hope that mass hysteria, wrong judgements and other only too human failings may be, if not corrected, at least understood. Let it be remembered, too, that the neighbourhood in which these characters live and work had at the time of the act – Murder? Manslaughter?

5

Execution? – been five years under the threat of a rapist's random violence.

ROBINA SANDEL, *fifty-six*

Lives at No. 19 Nightingale Crescent, which has been her home for over twenty years. Came to Britain from Austria at the outset of war. Runs her house as a boarding-house-cum-club for women. Her 'Mondays' have long been famous for the conversation, wit and good companionship of women – lawyers, doctors, architects, sometimes a visiting researcher with a Ph.D. thesis – and if some bear a grudge against Robina it's because the club is considered too exclusive and 'middle-class'. Those who do gain admittance speak highly of the Viennese *torte* – and of Robina's niece TILDA, who brings in Hock and seltzer just when it's needed.

MARA KALETSKY, *thirty*

Artist, film-maker, poet. Has an itinerant way of life, spending much of her time travelling (South America mostly, with troupes of actors and film crews) but at the time of events related here is staying at No. 19 Nightingale Crescent: ROBINA is an old friend, responsible some years before for saving MARA from a drugs bust in the notorious All Saints Road.

JEAN HASTIE, *thirty-four*

Was at school (Holland Park Comprehensive) a decade and a half ago with MARA and the two have kept in touch ever since. Latterly a practising solicitor, JEAN retired to look after husband and two small children in

6

Scotland in 1984. At MARA's invitation she is spending a short time in London, at ROBINA's. She has research to do on the Gnostic Gospels, at the British Library and the Fawcett Museum, for an illustrated book due for publication in 1989. She has also received a missive from a woman she knew slightly when she lived and worked in London after leaving school.

ELIZA JEKYLL *(age uncertain)*

Lives at No. 47 Nightingale Crescent. Has had various jobs (researcher for BBC, art publisher's assistant, etc.) and has now been appointed manageress of the Shade Gallery at 113a Portobello Road. The Shade Gallery has recently opened, and its first show, of photo-montage and oil-on-board artworks, is by MARA KALETSKY.

DR FRANCES CRANE, *forty-two*

Was a paediatrician at Great Ormond Street Hospital, now a GP. Specializes in diseases of the throat. Lives in a garden flat in Rudyard Crescent, on a long lease. DR CRANE is a frequent visitor to ROBINA SANDEL's house at No. 19 Nightingale Crescent. For an evening visit she is inclined to cut across the communal gardens and bang on ROBINA's back door, rather than go the long way round, via Ladbroke Grove.

MRS HYDE, *fifty-ish*

Lives in 99f, Ladbroke Grove, at a noisy junction, in a flat (basement) for which she has paid and continues to pay rent of £26.50 per week. The flat gives out on a small garden of its own, much neglected, which in turn gives out through a narrow passageway on to the gardens of Rudyard and Nightingale Crescents.

SIR JAMES LISTER, *forty-eight*

Financier and, amongst many other interests, proprietor of the Waldorf Gallery in Bond Street – and, latterly, the Shade Gallery, Portobello Road.

LADY LISTER

His wife.

TILDA

Niece of ROBINA SANDEL and working as a part-time *au pair* at No. 19 Nightingale Crescent while also attending an English course in South Kensington. She has recently arrived from her parents' home in Austria.

ROCK BOLT

Ex-rock star and recent purchaser of the freehold of 99 Ladbroke Grove.

ROGER

Gardener to the Rudyard/Nightingale Crescent gardens. Despite twenty-five years' work there, the residents take very little interest in him – with the exception of MS JEKYLL, who sometimes asks him in for a cup of tea and has given him permission to use her telephone.

PART ONE

The following reconstruction of events must begin on Monday the ninth of February, at the Shade Gallery in the Portobello Road.

Mara Kaletsky has been kind enough to let me view her video of the gallery opening party at noon on that day. The camera used is a Video 8, which has sync sound; unfortunately, though, as the camera was not functioning properly (a friend had lent it to her) Mara was not always able to obtain sound successfully, and some – possibly crucial – speeches are inaudible. The film, nevertheless, is worthy of inspection for two reasons:

1 It is one of the rare occasions when Eliza Jekyll can be seen without knowing she is seen, and may lead, therefore, to some insights into her personality useful to the examination demanded by the Executors of the late Dr Frances Crane.

2 The ensuing footage of Mrs Hyde may well prove invaluable to the case.

Mara Kaletsky's taped comments on her film are included here.

MARA KALETSKY'S VIDEO (*Voice-over*)

At first you'd think it was the wrong film.

Mahogany book-cases ... pillars of something that looks like Roman marble ... a fireplace wide and high enough to burn a Yule log ... all Heritage stuff in fact, and the funny part is that it's not two hundred yards from the most nefarious drugs den in all London, as well as the no-go area of All Saints Road, where the police have been clamping down on the blacks since anyone can remember.

Looks as if it's been there forever, doesn't it? But you could unclip that fireplace off the wall and stick it up in the hallway in any one of the new 'period' developments: it's a sort of instant respectability. Underneath ... there's just a hole in the wall and on the other side of it the Indian shop where the incense smell is so strong it seeps through and turns Sir James Lister's face quite purple with rage.

That's Sir James over there. He owns the gallery. He owns the massive new supermarket up by Kensal Road. He has houses all over the world and has just bought a country estate in Dorset. Yes, he is that colour, naturally, and there's nothing wrong with the film. Maybe it's port: he's limping slightly, as you can see, and perhaps he's got a simulated Heritage disease like gout from drinking it.

That's not the reason, though. I know why Sir James Lister limps. Now look at my canvases. I shoot film of all the women and I intercut the stills so I get the ultimate woman. You don't like that one? Who is it? It's the Face of Revenge. Look in the catalogue. No. 41. Two hundred and fifty pounds. Dirt cheap at the price and Sir James takes thirty per cent of that!

Very well, then, here's Eliza Jekyll herself. Here's the

official version, as the gallery is declared open by Sir James.

She looks lovely, doesn't she? If you fell for nothing else you'd fall for Eliza's hair. Thick ... glossy ... shining black hair. But everything about Eliza is pretty lovely. Her figure, for one thing ... and her beautiful mouth with that cherub's bow taken straight from the old movies and those Ingrid Bergman eyebrows. Here she is, smiling up at Sir James. And she hardly stiffens at all when the dirty old man slides his arm round her waist ... in that crêpe de Chine dress from Ungaro ... and keeps it there for the remainder of his speech. He looks like a toad opening and shutting his mouth like that, doesn't he?

Here's Robina Sandel, whose house I'm staying in.

Robina says she doesn't like my pictures. 'Mara!' (imitation of a German accent) 'Why you put so much *hate* in your vorrk? A preety girl like you ...' And I say, 'But, Robina, I'm only showing what so many women feel. Under the designer décor, if you know what I mean ...'

And this is her niece Tilda. Poor Tilda, who actually witnessed the dreadful deed. And worse, later. Don't these women understand that unless something is done, any man can feel free to be a rapist? How can she speak of love and hate, when things have got as bad as this?

*   *   *

Here the tape of Mara, as I recorded her on the subject of her film, breaks off. The camera, hand-held and wobbling violently, zooms in on a woman who looks distinctly out of place here: she's of medium height, wears a fawn mackintosh and has very short, curly hair that looks as if it's put into rollers at night. She's talking, surprisingly, to Eliza Jekyll – and they seem to have something very earnest to say to each other, as even without sound it's clear they're whispering with a good deal of urgency.

The camera, as if impatient of this acquaintanceship, veers off now to the main panel of pictures at the far end of the gallery. As it goes, there's a lurch and a sudden close-up of a red patch of fabric – and then it pulls back, having been handed to someone else to control while Mara grabs a bit of the limelight for herself. The woman in red, clearly no expert with this type of machine, succeeds in filming the skirt of her scarlet dress for several seconds before the exhibition and the gallery opening become once again the focus of the film.

Immediately it's easy to see why Mara 'puts people's backs up' – as I have heard Robina Sandel, loyal but disapproving, say. There's something provocative about her – it's almost as if she wants to invite some scandalous action and then draw attention to it. Though at this moment it's clear she's doing her best to show off – to attract any of the meagre number of men at the opening: perhaps she thinks Eliza Jekyll's immersion in conversation with Jean Hastie (as the curly-haired woman turned out to be) will leave the field free for her.

Not for the first time one is reminded of how frail – and how vulnerable – very small women like Mara can be. Possibly some of that vulnerability accounts for her pictures. They have a quality that is mesmerizing because it is, literally, indescribable: no single woman has those cheeks, that Cyclops eye, the turned-up nose

14

that adds a note of macabre humour to the Face of Revenge. And the unknown woman is herself spread over multi-panels so that a portion of her brooding, bruised face looks out with sudden ferocity from a corner of the gallery – or, again, a curtain of gold-silk hair with a gash of red torn flesh for a mouth looms from a suspended raft. There is too much pain to allow for an easy judgement – but two art critics (male) are staring up at the pictures with something very like fear and scorn – while Mara pirouettes, desperately craving attention.

Eliza Jekyll comes into frame here. She's laughing, stimulated by the party – though her manner does seem rather artificial – and on leaving her companion she comes up to Mara, smiles down at her small, twirling head and walks on, to disappear through a door marked Private at the rear of the room.

And now the film takes on a surreal tone of its own. Just as the camera is handed back to Mara – or she seizes it, impatient with the party (and thus, paradoxically, disappears from it, as far as the viewer is concerned) – the glass door into the Portobello Road is flung open and a crowd of women push in.

A flash; the sight of a plate-glass window smashing silently. Shards on the floor, large and bright like the tears frozen on the cheek of Mara's 'Madonna of the Gardens'. Chaos: a waitress drops a tray. Triangles of ham and smoked trout lie like skin debris after a bomb attack.

Then there's a burst of sound. I suppose at that point Mara, quite accidentally, must have got it to operate on the Video 8; and as the camera is wobbling all over the place by now, the screams of the guests make the scene all the more disturbing.

Now a voice, louder than the rest, authoritarian: Sir James Lister trying to control the mob. To no avail, though. It takes a woman's voice, quiet with a Scottish burr, to restore order to the gallery. 'I ask you all to stand by the door, please,' Jean Hastie says. 'And wait until the police arrive.'

A groan goes up. While the lens, uncertain still after the sputter of glass into the room, wanders over the faces of the women, it's possible to make out a feature here, a turn of the head there, an incline of the neck, which seem suddenly recognizable. Mara, who is by now leaning over to switch off the set, laughs at my perplexed expression. 'That's right,' she says. 'That was the Face of Revenge.'

The women were each one a part of her composite portrait, she said. And each had been a victim of rape.

'By the same man?' I asked.

'Oh yes.' Mara got up to stroll across my sitting room to french windows leading to the patio garden. She stood looking out at the white-washed walls and hanging baskets of geraniums and then moved restlessly away again. 'They were protesting . . . but not about my pictures, you understand. About the police and their attitude to the rapist. About a rich man like Sir James Lister and his ownership of their image . . .'

I interrupted, to ask if the women had planned the smashing of the window of the Shade Gallery in advance, or if it had been a spontaneous action. Mara burst out laughing again. 'What difference does it

16

make? She was there ... she always knew she was going to do it, probably.'

'She', as Mara Kaletsky explained as she picked up her equipment and slung everything into a dark blue bag, was Mrs Hyde. 'I saw her running away from the scene,' Mara reported, with another of those flirtatious laughs which seem to sum up her contradictory and puzzling character. 'She told me – she'd go and get the rapist herself next!'

AT ROBINA SANDEL'S

Robina Sandel was in the third-floor walk-in linen cupboard in her house in Nightingale Crescent when reports started to filter in about the gallery opening smash-up. Jean Hastie had come up the stairs and asked her some questions – mainly about Mrs Hyde, Robina remembers, who had apparently been the perpetrator of the outrage. 'I didn't know Jean Hastie before – she's an old friend of Mara Kaletsky's and Mara asked if she could come and stay here for a week while she was doing some research work or other – but what I do know is that she seems a bit too interested for my liking in what's going on round here. You'd think she was researching Communal Gardens rather than Original Sin!'

This reference to Jean Hastie's academic work (she is indeed preparing a book on Gnostic interpretations of the Garden of Eden) is typical of Robina Sandel's sharp, scathing sense of humour. People say it's a pity she didn't do as so many of her compatriots did – go to America – Hollywood – and make movies about contemporary mores, dressed up as a comedy or melo-drama. 'Like Billy Wilder – or Douglas Sirk,' says Mara, a passionate admirer of these directors. 'But, of course, as a woman, how could she?'

All of which is probably true; but for my own pur-poses Robina, with her combination of voyeurism and Brechtian indignation, makes a perfect witness to the horrifying events of that February. Her inner eye, accus-tomed from childhood to the art of Grosz and the Expressionists, was the first to see, I believe, the logical outcome of an impossible political and psychological situation and its manifestation in one individual; and all that seems strange in retrospect is that an onlooker – more, a participant in these events, such as Jean Hastie – should have been oblivious to the underlying dangers of the situation.

Robina said she'd hardly known any two friends more unalike than Mara and Jean. It wasn't just that one was big – plump, even – and with those tight curls that were just about as far from Mara's rough, shaggy mane of dark hair as Jean's 'court' shoes were from the espad-rilles Mara wore night and day on her small feet; it was the manner of thinking: the approach to life. 'Mara is sorry for everyone, you know.' (Robina does have a German accent, but not nearly so pronounced as Mara makes out in her mimicry.) 'Mara would take any lame duck that comes up in front of her. And – my God – there are plenty of those around nowadays.' Jean Hastie, on the other hand, seemed unmoved by the obvious changes in London since she had last come south of the border, several years ago. 'She's got a happy family life, I suppose,' Robina said, with a sigh that was immediately succeeded by a warm, enigmatic smile – most of Robina Sandel's family had been lost to Nazi Germany; and she had never married. 'But they've nothing in common – she and Mara. Funnily enough, they seem simply to like each other's company.'

That this was the case was proved by Mara's and Jean Hastie's late return from the gallery opening. Jean Hastie calmed Mara when she was in one of her 'states' – Robina Sandel conceded that – and after the smashing of the window and the arrival of the mob of angry women, Mara had certainly needed a gentle touch. 'She's torn both ways,' Robina said shortly. 'On the one hand, Mara wants people to buy her paintings – and to appreciate her as an artist. On the other, she's chosen to paint a very sensitive subject: the victims of the local Ripper. She wants the approval and patronage of such as Sir James Lister. Yet she would like to send him to the guillotine.' Robina chuckled in a manner, I thought, that would irritate Jean Hastie intensely, if she was truly lacking in pity and indulgence for others as had been described. Friendship, however, is an imponderable thing; and certainly, when the two women came back from a walk round Holland Park, Mara had recovered herself and was able to laugh at the whole thing quite good-naturedly.

'I was just sorting the sheets,' Robina said. 'I'd told Tilda to give Frances Crane – who'd just come across the gardens for a drink and a chat – she visits us about three times a week – a malt whisky from our supply. I had to make the bed up for Jean Hastie in a hurry because the other spare room has a young architect friend of mine – she's been in Brasilia for the past six months and she

19

needs a good rest here and some nice food . . .'

Robina Sandel is inclined to get side-tracked in this way when it comes to domestic arrangements. It's almost as if, Mara pointed out, she has made the running of the house, the serving of meals, and the secrets of the linen cupboard a whole State, with all the importance and changes of policy which Government requires. Whether this was really the 'tragedy' that Mara claims, of the loss of a brilliant talent – so common a fate among women – and its submersion in the mundane details of everyday life, I wouldn't be able to say; I only know that it took some time to return Robina to the subject of the evening of Monday the ninth of February. It wasn't, as she was eager to explain, because there had been so many guests since then that the occasion had dimmed in her mind. 'No – if anything, that week burns itself all the time more deeply in my memory,' Robina said.

Nor was it just that the search for Mrs Hyde, as notorious by now as the absconding Lord Lucan in his day, was a part of the national consciousness. It was, Robina said, her own sense of shame – blame others though she might – at having been unable to predict the day of the murder. 'The Zeitgeist is not to my liking,' she said, rueful but with an intimation once more of the enigmatic look and smile. 'I don't like the priggish Jean Hastie – and I don't like the viragos poor Mara has got caught up with. All the fault of men. I cannot believe that. However –' Robina became her sharp self again and delivered one of her fatally glancing comments. 'A snoop is always a snoop. That is what I thought of Jean Hastie.'

Apparently Frances Crane, already ensconced in Robina Sandel's shabby 'through' room overlooking the gardens, got on well with Jean from the start. Frances, as a doctor – and a specialist in the ailments of children – had enough in her working day, I suppose, of an 'immature' approach to things, to find Mara a little trying and Jean Hastie a welcome relief. Whatever the reason, the two women were soon settled on a battered leather sofa by the window. It was a horribly dark night, as Robina Sandel remembers, and she had gone so far as to light a candle and place it on a low table by the new acquaintances. It was one of those fat Christmas candles – her niece Tilda had brought it over from Austria when she came – and the flame, reflected in the window, showed up the gloom of a February afternoon only too well, the bare chestnut tree and forked ash outside groaning and straining in a deathly parody of the leaping light inside. There was a lot of rain – Mara remembers that because later she tried to film in the gardens and was blown back in again, soaked – and a wind that seemed to be trapped in the stretch between Rudyard and Nightingale Crescents, howling round, as Robina said with that Germanic, ghoulish humour, 'like a woman or a lost soul'.

Jean Hastie was asking Frances about Eliza Jekyll, whose gallery opening she had just witnessed. (Robina says that at this point two 'regulars' of No. 19 came in and made themselves comfortable at the street end of the room, with a bottle of claret produced by Tilda.) These details are essential, I believe, as the new arrivals, one a stockbroker who had lived in her ground-floor flat four houses down for six years, and the other a landscape gardener only recently arrived to take up a studio flat with private garden on the far side of the communal expanse, in Rudyard Crescent, were witnesses to subsequent events. Robina remembers that the stockbroker, Monica Purves, lit up a cigar and pulled one of the giant brass ashtrays Tilda has to keep polished close to her on the coffee table between them. Jean Hastie, who seems to have had a particularly strong sense of smell, wrinkled her nose at this, despite being at the far end of the room from them, and asked if a window could be opened somewhere.

'I suppose', Robina said, 'that that was where the trouble started. Two factions, if you like, declared themselves at that moment and stayed implacably opposed until they were forced to part – by the lateness of the hour, the necessity of getting up and going to work the next morning – or the sheer weariness that overcomes an argument when it finally becomes clear that neither side will budge an inch.' It was then, Robina emphasized, that grounds for her suspicions of Jean Hastie were first properly laid; and though she could never have guessed, as she was the first to point out, the exact nature of Mrs Hastie's mission in the south, there was something of an air of espionage about her. And Robina didn't like that at all.

The inevitable subject of the local rapist having come up (the four women were sitting together, now, since Monica Purves's offer to open the side window at the rear end of the room, with its pitch black view of boarding and sodden shrub, had brought them all to the garden end of the room) it soon led on to the topic of women in general; and the change (if any) in society's attitude to physical violence and social discrimination against them. Monica Purves, still puffing on her cigar, put her legs in pinstriped trousers up on the brass fender (another of Tilda's polishing tasks) that guarded the fine old wooden fireplace at the garden end of the room. There was a log fire burning, Robina said, because a number of trees had blown down a few weeks ago and Monica had sawn them up and brought them round. It was about the time, as she remembered very well, of the rapist's last attack in the area. Someone had grabbed his sleeve – they'd got as near as that to catching him! – and he'd got away all the same, dodging through the copse of silver birches on the western side (where the land was boggy and wet, this time of year, and residents didn't let their children play) and out into the street, somehow. A shred of a bomber jacket had been left behind, Robina added, on a branch of an ash that had gone down later in the storms. Monica had enjoyed ceremonially burning it in the fireplace of No. 19.

The conversation, as if drawn by a momentum of its own, now moved to the nature of Ms Jekyll, followed by a heated appraisal of the nature of Mrs Hyde. It was strange, Robina reflected, that the characteristics of these two women, barely known to anyone present, should have brought a civilized talk almost to boiling point; but that it did was incontrovertible; it was as if, she said, these two not particularly newsworthy characters stood for all the divisions we are in the midst of suffering in this country. 'I don't know who really began it,' Robina went on to say, 'but you can bet your bottom dollar it was something Mara said that got someone's hackles up in the first place.'

As far as one can make out, the argument was well under way before the incident, as poor Tilda, frightened out of her wits, termed it, of 'the ghost in the garden'. Mara had spoken with derision of Eliza Jekyll – typical of Mara, as her friends will say sorrowfully – for her contradictory character likes to bite the hand that feeds it. 'Eliza is the kind of woman who gives women a bad name,' Mara said. She was perched by now on the leather top of the fender, Monica Purves's black expensive-looking lace-ups crossed beside her. 'She's the kind of woman who believes she is a post-feminist. Whatever that means. Except I'll tell you what it means – getting what you want in the old way while pretending you care for equality and other old-fashioned concepts. A fink, in other words.'

Robina put in a word here, before things got heated (or rather, she hoped to deflect the confrontation). Already the young landscape gardener, Carol Hill, was shifting restlessly in the upright chair next to Jean Hastie's and Frances Crane's armchairs. Jean herself, catching the look in the gardener's eye, was shaking her head vehemently.

'I don't agree,' Monica Purves said. 'Eliza Jekyll is an example of a woman achieving in the world without losing her basic feelings of compassion towards humanity. Did you know, for example, that Eliza is a sponsor of the local Homeless Women Trust? She organizes meetings for Legacy for the Homeless, where an elderly person may will his or her house to the Foundation, and benefit from tax relief in the meantime – '

'Yes. And personally as well,' Carol Hill put in. 'Since I moved into my flat here I've heard the children these homeless women bring round, playing all day in Eliza's flat. Surely that counts for more than just attending meetings?'

'Soon you'll be telling me she's running a Green Investment Trust, where the rich can put their money in wild flowers or butterflies or something,' Mara snapped at the stockbroker. 'Capitalism is the cause of Eliza Jekyll's prosperity. And capitalism will continue to bring her prosperity while others starve.'

It was at this point that Jean Hastie spoke up. Her voice, with its quiet burr, wasn't easily audible at first – and Dr Frances Crane, who had been sitting back during this exchange with a slightly worried expression on her face, held up her hand to stop the next bass outburst from Monica Purves. 'Jean came down from Scotland to see Eliza, I believe,' Frances Crane said, 'as well as researching for your book, isn't that right?' And she turned to her new friend with an almost apologetic expression on her face – as if the state of affairs in London was indeed very different from that obtaining in the fresher air north of the border.

'I haven't seen Eliza Jekyll for many years,' Jean said quietly, when Mara, too, had been persuaded to hold her tongue. 'We were at the same digs once – at Headington Hill, outside Oxford – '

'Digs!' Mara couldn't restrain a snort of laughter. 'That sounds pretty antediluvian to me. So you didn't know her when she was married, then?'

'Married?' Jean Hastie turned in her chair. 'I didn't even know – '

'It didn't last long,' Frances Crane put in quickly, as if already trying to protect her recently found ally. 'He – the man she married, I mean – has been living out of the country for years.' And, with a disapproving glance in Mara's direction, she said, 'I really can't see what Eliza Jekyll's marital status has got to do with this conversation.'

'I agree.' Monica Purves tossed the end of her cheroot into the fireplace and stood up. 'A friend of a friend of mine did her divorce, as a matter of fact. The trouble was, she said, that Eliza Jekyll was a lot too soft on the bastard. Let him get away with murder, old Kate said.'

Robina's account is that she went at this point to replenish the drink tray and to call Tilda in the kitchen. Robina is proud of the mini-pizzas she hands out to those who drop in at No. 19; and if they dig a little deeper in their pockets for the extras, all the better. Certainly Monica Purves had no lack of funds, as Robina rather shamefacedly said. With London the way it is nowadays, you can do with every bob you earn. And as if unconsciously to underline a 'decent' way of thinking and talking that had, like Jean Hastie's memories of a distant past when Eliza had been studying art at a school in Oxford and Jean had been studying law, long disappeared, Robina added apologetically that No. 19 did, after all, need a new roof. You couldn't tell these days if you were always going to have a roof over your head, when it came down to it. The house might be hers – but for how long could you borrow against its very fabric, eating into walls and foundations as you struggled to stay on?

When the reasons for the providing of tasty snacks

and charging for them had been gone through – for Robina was a hospitable character and didn't like to charge her regulars at all, when she sat and drank with them as well – the rest of the story of that evening was permitted to proceed. She'd found Tilda in the small room off the basement kitchen where she'd been temporarily housed since the arrival of a paying guest, Jean Hastie, who would take Tilda's room in the mansard extension at the top of the house. Robina's niece was packing up her things in a big hold-all and choking back tears as she did so. A tray of pizzas gave off a particularly pungent burnt smell from the oven next door, Robina said, and at first she imagined the girl was crying because she was guilty at having neglected them. Then she saw that matters were more serious than that. Tilda was afraid, she said. It was that woman Mrs Hyde who had frightened her. And the other woman, too – Mara Kaletsky, with her wild talk of revenge and her gruesome descriptions of the methods of the rapist. She said Mrs Hyde was going to kill the man. It would be soon, Mara said. At the time of his next attack. She had told Tilda to be very careful. 'But even if you're not in he cuts up your things,' Tilda sobbed. 'Your photos ... your underwear ... every-thing.'

It next turned out that Tilda had come down to the basement to fetch the appetizers when she had seen, through the open door of her bedroom, a pile of old clothes in a tangle on the floor. Heightened imagination – fear – 'well, they can do a lot to the way you see something,' as Robina, no innocent in these matters, remarked drily. She added, remembering perhaps the country she had left and the growth and easy acceptance of fear there when she had been a child younger than Tilda, that she'd thought then how good it would be if something – anything almost – would just remove the menace of the rapist from their midst. 'It's been a long time,' as she told the newspaper reporters when, inevitably, they came to prise a 'story' from her three days later. And – as if her niece's accommodation had anything to do with the whole grisly affair: 'I wouldn't have put Tilda downstairs, you understand, if a friend of Mara's, Jean Hastie, hadn't been coming to stay. Tilda was upstairs all the time since she came to England. I just moved her down until . . .' At this point Robina Sandel's voice, or the transcript obtainable from the *Recorder*, dies out altogether. Did she really think she was in some way responsible for the events which succeeded the evening of the ninth of February? Everyone knew, of course, that she was not. But guilt and hysteria, brought back in one long gulp from Robina's childhood, made a confession of a simple domestic transfer of rooms. (It's possible, some say, that it was the presence of Tilda – the sight of her in the basement room, maybe, when she stood by Robina's cheap pink unlined curtains, that brought things to a head that week. But how can it ever be proved? And, if Tilda's stay below stairs was indeed the catalyst, wasn't some kind of action exactly what was wanted then . . . as Robina Sandel had been the first to say?)

* * *

MARA'S FILM

Maybe it was because everyone seemed to be against Mara Kaletsky that evening – with the possible exception of the landscape gardener, Carol Hill, seen to be moved by Mara's vehement defence of Mrs Hyde – that the young film-maker and artist decided to go ahead with her 'project', despite the appalling climatic conditions, claiming afterwards that she had known all along what she would find out there in the gardens.

The door leading from the passage to the flight of wooden steps outside had blown open in the wind; and this caused, as far as one can make out, a quite uncontrollable sensation of panic and hysteria among the women. You could practically feel the fear, Robina said; and Mara going out through that door, leaving it to bang behind her in the wind, didn't help matters at all. It was as if a collective terror was brewing, and was responsible, perhaps, for turning the ordinary sight of an ordinary woman into a vision of particular horror.

In Robina Sandel's opinion, the phenomena undoubtedly witnessed could be laid fair and square at the door of her niece, Tilda. Not necessarily known as a superstitious woman, Robina was soon talking of poltergeists; and if Dr Freud had been brought into the picture as well, he would probably have been the first to agree with Robina's other diagnosis, that Tilda's psychic state was due to her recent shock in the basement (where, it went without saying, she had left her clothes untidily herself, the mess being in no way the responsibility of the prowler or other invader) and that the state in which she now found herself was in all likelihood due to an innate guilt on the subject of untidiness, imbued in her by a mother who suffered from 'Housewife's Neurosis'.

However it was looked at, Robina stressed, Tilda

came up those stairs from the basement as white as a sheet and shaking. Robina followed with a few of the pizzas she had been able to rescue. It was as if, she said, Tilda's shaking whiteness had been translated to some denizen of another world – for as she came in, the candle flame swerved wildly and went out (the electric lights had been extinguished by Monica Purves at an earlier point in the fireside chat) and a 'white thing', as Tilda screamed on first seeing it, appeared outside Robina's long windows overlooking the gardens of Rudyard and Nightingale Crescents.

Mara's film shows us at this point the appearance of Mrs Hyde – on the evening of Monday the ninth of February at 6 p.m. at least – and should prove an invaluable aide to the police in their search.

Mara's desire to film Mrs Hyde, and, as she said, some kind of weird instinct, led her to go out in the gardens at the most unpropitious time and aim her Video 8 at a path and shrubbery turned almost upside down by a seemingly unending squall. Her hair was standing on end, she admitted – and the sight from the garden of the women in Robina Sandel's drawing room, wide-eyed and open-mouthed – clearly seeing something she had not seen herself – was hardly reassuring. She'd heard, though, that Mrs Hyde on certain evenings would make a tour of the gardens in the hope of catching the man who had for so long held the neighbourhood in terror; she would avenge her sisters, Mara had been told; and this was an essential face for a new photo-montage devoted to women's resistance to oppression.

If Mara hadn't seen the woman approach, the camera had.

Robina Sandel, I believe, best summed up the responses to the apparition of Mrs Hyde on that stormy evening, and perhaps it's because they're so much at odds with each other and with what the viewfinder actually saw, that we should listen to her.

Tilda, of course, saw a ghost. This white 'thing', which humped round the gardens in a drench of rain so fine it was almost a steam, came straight from the subterranean world. Clinging to her aunt, she cried that she wanted to go home.

There was certainly nothing homely about the sight of Mrs Hyde that evening. Disgusted, possibly, by an unwelcome combination of the familiar and the unknown – for the 'thing' wore nothing more alarming than a white mac, one of those plastic, half-transparent coats with a hood that sell in millions – Jean Hastie commented that 'it was odious that a woman should disport herself in a respectable area such as this' – and was oblivious, apparently, to the unsuitability of the weather or the possibly unhinged state of mind of the walker. For Jean, the sartorial appearance of Mrs Hyde – for she wore nothing, it was true, under the diaphanous white plastic – was alarming and all-important, blinding her to anything else.

For Monica Purves disgust and alarm are expressed in economic terms. Her view is that women like Mrs Hyde could easily support themselves 'if they really wanted to': that 'making an exhibition of yourself' by parading in cheap and common clothing on a night such as this is done to draw attention to your straitened circumstances. If her wish was to catch the rapist, Monica Purves said, she would be unlikely to succeed. He would hardly be tempted out in a storm of rain by Mrs Hyde's unattractive get-up, to pounce in full view of other residents of the gardens.

Carol Hill's response differs drastically. She has heard from Mara that by now Mrs Hyde is shortly to be evicted from her premises in Ladbroke Grove. Her two small children are frequently ill (all this information passed on to the susceptible Mara by 'the *tricoteuses*', as Robina Sandel nervously describes those women who have banded together in the wake of the rapist's attacks to express their rage and dissatisfaction with society). Carol sees a woman hounded to the limits of her sanity by the brutality of everyday life.

Only Frances Crane and the camera are equally silent on their view of Mrs Hyde that night; both, perhaps, are equally revealing in their silence.

The lens shows us a face that seems almost to have stopped being a face altogether. It's as if a once wide-boned, generous face, a beautiful face, even, to go by the high bridge of a slender nose and the curve of the jaw, has in some indescribable way been pulled sideways and downwards – so that an evil, spiteful face, a nose hooked like a witch's in the old pictures, eyes baleful and peering in a cloud of rain that's like the rising mists of a Hell that lies always at her feet – looks back at us in Mara's version. Robina Sandel is right, I think, when she says that the extreme unease experienced by all the women in their different ways when confronted by this spectacle is due to there being something 'unnatural' about Mrs Hyde. Possibly, as a doctor,

Frances Crane feels that comments on physical appearance due to evident malnutrition, stress and (although not proven) advanced alcoholism or drug-taking, would not be ethical in the circumstances.

It was after Mara Kaletsky had come inside once more that the argument resumed – its subject having gone round the gardens for the last time and disappeared in the direction of Ladbroke Grove.

The weighing of the disadvantages of this woman's situation against the advantages of a woman like Eliza Jekyll, in present-day society, went on until the small hours, for the simple reason, Robina thinks, that the women in her house that night were ashamed of their earlier fear and wanted to exorcize it with a strong, political discussion.

As Robina commented, it would be hard to know quite where Jean Hastie stood in the dispute over the 'new values', for, while she appeared to disapprove strongly of Mrs Hyde and the predicament in which the 'feckless' woman had placed herself, the solicitor from Scotland seemed almost equally disapproving of some aspect of another kind relating to Ms Eliza Jekyll. As the argument raged, the storm moaned outside with a tedium that made Robina think – and here she is wandering way off track again – of a reputedly haunted room in a castle in Jean Hastie's country, where card-players, gambling till dawn with the Devil, are all of a sudden whisked off to eternity, the sound of their laughter and revels remaining behind on wild nights to frighten poor sleepers. She would gladly have locked all her women guests in her sitting room until such time as the Evil One came to get them, Robina goes on, laughing. But, however that may be, there wasn't a soul there – professional, independent, self-reliant though all (with the exception of poor Tilda) indeed were – who had not been scared out of their wits that evening.

To discover further some of the reasons for Jean Hastie's ambiguous attitude to her old friend of student days, Ms Eliza Jekyll, it is necessary to read some at least of that good woman's journal for her stay in London while researching a book on the Gnostic Gospels and the origins of sin.

* * *

JEAN HASTIE'S JOURNAL

Tuesday, Feb. 10th

I consider myself a feminist. And I hope to contribute, with my work of gynocriticism *In the Garden*, to the controversy surrounding the very roots of the phallocracy in which women have been forced to live since the beginning of recorded history. Painstaking historical research, I believe, is the only sure path away from prejudice and towards a new state of equality at all levels between the sexes.

I must say here, therefore, that I am quite painfully shocked by the atmosphere and general behaviour of old friends and acquaintances as I have found them in London after a period of five years away. A combination of emotional insecurity and extreme aggression appears to be the norm here; and as for the possibility of efforts being made in a balanced manner to redress the economic-social disadvantages which remain, for women, all traces of an attempt at this appear to have been replaced by my own particular bugbear – monomania.

I hadn't met Monica Purves before – and it's possible that I'm simply out of date when it comes to lesbian activists, their aims and means of expression. And Carol Hill, the youthful Capability Brown of the Crescent Gardens, seems as easily swayed by one opinion or the other as she would be if offered varying fashions in the laying out of a parterre or pergola.

But Mara! – I am sad indeed to see the degeneration into bathos of one of the brightest sparks one was ever likely to know. I was literally horrified yesterday to see the outpouring of hatred and desire for vengeance in the canvases at the Shade Gallery. What can have overcome her? (There are still traces of the old Mara there, of course, and on our walk in Holland Park after the fracas at the gallery I was briefly allowed to savour them. She and I were reminiscing about the old days, when we shared the big flat in Elvaston Place – Mara was experimenting with colour then and great daubs appeared on the walls – 'That's a Rothko and that's a Frank Stella,' Mara would say laughing, before sponging them off again. And we had a laugh remembering Andy, who used to come round too often in pursuit of Mara and one night got drunk and ate the dog's bowl of Chum before passing out.) There was something more innocent about those days, I suppose . . . anyway, we were having a good time remembering all this until we got to Robina Sandel's and last night's chilling and absurd little melodrama was played out.

No doubt I am extremely fortunate to have a kind and

loyal husband in Fife, two happy children, and a good income coming in from Paul's work in Edinburgh, where he commutes every day. And I know, from Mara's letters over the past few years – and sometimes we've gone a whole year without corresponding, Mara caught up in the internecine politics of Women's Agitprop and Art of one sort or another, and I sampling the exhausting but rewarding fruits of childbearing – that I'm considered by now a bit of a fuddy-duddy. Mara's view is that because I trained as a solicitor I should practise still as a solicitor, whether I have a young family or not. I should be helping women in their legal battles – against absconding, non-maintenance-paying husbands, against wife-batterings, in rape cases and the like. I'm seen to have let down the side, I fear, and Mara's letters, friendly but increasingly exasper-ated, accuse me of being a Women's Institute type who makes home-made preserves and crochets table mats for the Church sale.

Mara is right there and I'm sorry to say I can't feel apologetic about it. I prefer to raise my children in the calm, sane atmosphere of the countryside rather than in the frenetic drug-ridden inner cities. And I can't see anything wrong with making our own produce: both Karen and Allan enjoy our bilberry-picking expeditions and enjoy it, too, when covered with purple stains at the time of making the jelly.

Paul was quite happy to make arrangements in Edinburgh so that I could come south to visit the British Library for a week. I miss the bairns, of course – but I would feel that I was not making my contribution to the women's cause if I allowed the contingencies of motherhood to take me away from my work more than absolutely necessary.

Then, too, I have to admit that I was intrigued to receive a letter from Eliza Jekyll just a few weeks ago.

It really is centuries since I last saw Eliza. Those days in Oxford seem to belong to another age altogether. So it was particularly surprising to be asked a favour – as Eliza put it. She hinted that my legal training would in some way come in useful. But I was mystified as to what a woman in the centre of metropolitan life – and a woman who, as I heard last night, had married and divorced (and all without my legal aid) – could want of me when solicitors, barristers and influential friends must abound in her life.

I was most concerned when, arriving off the Edinburgh shuttle at Heathrow – to be met by Mara in her same old bashed-up Beetle car – and taken directly to the gallery in Portobello Road, Eliza took me aside and told me the nature of her request.

Now, my view in these matters is that, while the State should on no account be expected to provide lesbian play centres and the like out of tax-payers' money, and that prevailing attitudes towards a self-help ethos are highly commendable, the limits of philanthropy of an individual nature should also be carefully guarded. Charity may come in the wake of a cutting back of Government support for those unable or unwilling to help themselves. But it should not, most emphatically, fall into the trap of the quixotic.

This was just how Eliza struck me last night at the Shade Gallery – and that was before the appalling revelations which followed the opening. She had a superficial air about her that I don't remember from our student days – but, I must say, she looked remarkably unchanged since then, as if the cares and wrinkles that beset the rest of us, had, magically, eluded her. She seemed a bit jittery, too, but I put that down to gallery opening nerves – and I gathered from Sir James Lister that the place has only just been renovated and launched as a picture gallery; and that it's the first time he has employed Eliza, who a few weeks ago he didn't know at all. Certainly I had a slight feeling that the young woman I'd known when a student of Art History was less in touch with the banalities of real life now than she, very clearly, had been at Oxford. (For if Mara, for example, had always had this wild, romantic side to her character – a true 'artistic personality', I suppose you could say – then Eliza, despite her good looks, was always extremely down to earth.) Her only fault, as I remember it, was generosity – she once gave her entire term's allowance to a student who was down on his luck, and worked at the Cardrona Tea Rooms to pay her way through her studies.

That, as I discovered, was the simple fact of the matter: as often happens over the years, a charming quality – such as generosity – can develop into an unattractive, even embarrassing characteristic. I'm no psychoanalyst, but it does occur to me that some need to control the lives of others is concomitant with an obsessive need to make gifts; and an apparent need to dominate the exist-ence of another seemed to be uppermost in Eliza's mind as she spoke to me yesterday in the gallery. It was, of course, not for me to say so at the time – and our exchange was necessarily brief – but charity should surely, in Eliza's case, permit her to remain in her own home.

For it transpires that Eliza Jekyll wishes me to act as a conveyancer for her. She wishes – no less – to give her home away.

And my horror can be imagined when, in the course of the evening at Robina Sandel's, I understood the nature of the intended recipient.

It was none other than Mrs Hyde.

* * *

London Transport has certainly worsened considerably since I was last here and the effect of my journey to the British Library and the long wait for the volumes I needed has been to make me yearn for sleep.

But I think I should record here – for Paul, who will doubtless be intrigued to listen when I return to an account of the excesses of the sybaritic southern flesh-pots – the efforts I have made so far on behalf of my friend Eliza Jekyll.

It has come home to me with increasing strength that Eliza must be in some kind of trouble. Possibly she's being blackmailed – for a distant indiscretion, which if made public now would jeopardize her future career. (I must admit, in this age of Gomorrah, I cannot imagine what this could be!) Perhaps some problem with her ex-husband has led her into a legal tangle over her Nightingale Crescent flat.

Again, it is hard to imagine what this could be. But it's equally hard to believe that a propensity such as

Eliza's in her salad days could have grown to a monster of such suicidal and self-sacrificial dimensions.

I may be doubly cautious, as a Scot, when it comes to keeping a roof over my head. But it's not been in my experience, in all my years as a solicitor, that anyone renders themselves intentionally homeless.

No, there's something afoot here. I shall seek it out, for Eliza's sake and in the interests of justice.

And I must push to the back of my mind the pre-posterous thought that there was indeed at some time a relationship between Eliza and that – that literally indescribable creature I witnessed humping round the communal gardens last night.

Quite honestly, if there was or had been, necrophilia would have been the only word for it. For Mrs Hyde, as the wretched eighteen-year-old German girl put it, was as alarming and repellent in appearance as a ghost. This other-worldliness was what, I think, caused the bout of mass panic at Robina Sandel's. A woman going round the gardens in the wind and the rain. And she looked like death.

* * *

I was glad to meet Dr Frances Crane last night. And I'm only sorry that we didn't end up getting on as well as we began. After Robina Sandel – who is a bit of an eavesdropper and a busybody (always seems to be hanging around just when you think she's finally gone off to do something; and the bossiness, too, when she told me I had to move downstairs to the room off the kitchen, although I know Mara had arranged for me to have the light, airy room at the top!) – after Robina had settled us with a drink and a low table with some sort of expensive-looking candle on it, I was at last able to ask the doctor what if anything she knew about Eliza Jekyll. Mara had told me they were old friends, and it was funny timing, I said, that this relic of my student days turned out to live in the same street as Mara: that all these years Mara and I had corresponded from her 'temporary' London address in Robina's house, Eliza had been there just a few doors along.

'A lot of people seem to end up round here,' Dr Crane said, with a careful smile, as if she would guard any secrets with extreme punctiliousness. 'It's the gardens, I suppose. There isn't another area in London with such an acreage of open green spaces.'

I had the feeling I was never going to get any further than this with Dr Frances Crane. And yet she had obviously felt an instinctive liking for me as I had for her. Perhaps the wildness of Mara and the opinionated manner of Monica Purves made me appear a more restful companion for an evening's relaxation after a day's hard work than they were likely to be; possibly, recognizing a fellow professional, she felt she could count on my discretion if the time did come to let out some facts.

I was to be disappointed again, however. Dr Crane seemed more interested in the fact that Eliza Jekyll's ex-husband was in town (which of course could be of no conceivable interest to me) than in her old friend. 'I heard from a patient,' Frances said unhelpfully. 'Many of the mothers of my young charges seem to have met and fallen for Ed. I sometimes wonder if the illnesses the children contract aren't in some way connected with the mothers' infatuation.' And the doctor, seeing my surprise, went on to explain that Eliza's ex-husband was a famous charmer, an occasional film director, who led a charmed life, too, by the sound of it, living off 'projects' in development money and, often as not, the rich and famous. When in London, this paragon of virtue stays at the Portobello Hotel; and as Dr Crane has her practice in the area, she is inclined to be the first to know when he has arrived, due, as she had just explained, to the symptoms manifest in the children of single mothers living on their own, Ed's chosen love-partners.

He sounds not unlike the rapist, I thought, but kept my thoughts to myself. If I was ever going to get some insight into the unrealistic bequest Eliza Jekyll had in mind, I would do well to listen to anything anyone chose to tell me, however irrelevant.

'So he goes to see Eliza fairly often?' I said.

'Oh, I shouldn't think so,' Dr Crane said, returning my look of surprise. 'He treated her monstrously at the time of the divorce.' Frances Crane sighed, then turned to look down the far end of the room, where a new arrival was lighting a great cigar – a habit I feel strongly should be banned by Robina Sandel if she wishes to keep a pleasant establishment here.

'Eliza's attitude to life is beyond me, I'm afraid. It's a good time since we met,' were the woman doctor's last and distinctly disapproving words on the subject. And so strong was the feeling of dislike – of dread, almost – on Frances Crane's part when talking of her old friend, that I called out for a window to be opened: ostensibly to clear the room of the fumes from the cigar, but in fact to clear the sudden thundery air between us. Eliza Jekyll would yield none of her secrets through the intermediary of the doctor, that was plain. But, in one last hope that the mystery of the contract she wished me to draw up could be elucidated, I decided to ask the doctor if she had ever had dealings with a certain Mrs Hyde.

Again, I drew a blank. Frances Crane looked up from her deep leather armchair in the bay and waved at the woman who had just come over to open the side window at my request, inviting her and her young friend to come and join us. As they settled themselves, the older and taller of the two women leaning back in a low tapestry–covered seat and propping her legs on the brass fender, Dr Crane shook her head in a dismissive, almost impatient way.

'The woman who I hear was responsible for smashing the window of the Shade Gallery this afternoon,' I reminded her, 'or incited the other women to smash it.'

I suppose I must sometimes come over as an insensitive person. There has been difficulty in the past, on occasions, with particularly obdurate clients – those who were manifestly holding back information from me. I have been accused of lack of tact and sympathy with their predicament. But it is a long time since I have received a snub so direct and wounding as the one delivered to me by Dr Frances Crane on the occasion of my innocent inquiries apropos Mrs Hyde. I have my book to write, and other matters to think about than the property transfers of someone with whom I have had no contact for over twenty years. I am invited to dine – with Mara – at Eliza's on Thursday, and no doubt we will find time to discuss her request more rationally then.

Such at least were the thoughts that went through my mind after Dr Crane's glacial reply. 'I fear, Mrs Hastie,' she said, 'that I cannot satisfy your curiosity. My friendships do not lie in that domain.' And she turned to talk animatedly to the young woman, a landscape gardener, who had just come with the taller woman to sit down beside us. An argument on the merits and disadvantages of conservatories ensued: too hot in summer, according to the doctor, and encouraging sunstroke in some of her infant patients; and too cold in winter to be of any comfort.

I resolved not to sit silent and humiliated while this tedious conversation went on. It had been a long day, the flight from Edinburgh and the strain of parting from my children not to be discounted. And Mara – wandering out to the passage with that video camera in her hand – if I could just separate her from it for tonight, we could have a cosy chat in our rooms before turning in.

But then, of course, we got our Lady Macbeth sleepwalking scene.

After it was over – and the argument had veered as sharply as the candle flame in the wind from the pros and cons of conservatories to the cons (mostly) of Mrs Hyde, it was appallingly late.

And I wouldn't have been able to have a bedside chat with Mara, anyway. I'd temporarily forgotten that Robina had moved all my things down to a poky, most unwelcoming basement room.

* * *

LOOKING FOR MRS HYDE

It seems unlikely that Jean Hastie's long – overlong – account of her days in the British Library could be of much value here. Yet, though her research on the subject of Original Sin was, of course, of paramount importance to her, the journal, maddeningly incomplete just where the strict and meticulous attention to detail, for which the Scottish lawyer had always been remarked, would have been most appreciated, does at the same time show an undeniable urge to seek out the evil Mrs Hyde. Jean was determined – as she rather inappositely put it – to beard her in her den.

A frustrating day on Wednesday the eleventh of February prompted Jean Hastie to leave her desk by the middle of the afternoon. The books and manuscripts she most wanted were out to someone else – and for a historian in the rich field of women's studies this might well mean a further list of scholars equally impatient to study the Gospels – and an impulse to visit the London Library with a card of introduction from Robina Sandel became, as a grey, rainy twilight descended, increasingly easy to resist. The streets, where orange shop windows beckoned with displays more extravagant and sumptuous than those to be found north of the border, seemed to lie like arms a-glitter with bangles and rings, from the vantage point of the Library window; and Mrs Hastie, as much lured by the prospect of vicarious shopping as the possibility of escape from an unfruitful period of research, went out to meet them with a sense both of purpose and relief. Soon, after a concentrated walk in the bustle and dazzle of Oxford Street and Piccadilly Circus, she found herself, by way of a No. 15 bus, approaching the less salubrious parts of Notting Hill.

Everyone has heard their own version of the impossible coincidence, the chance meeting that is a million to one against. A favourite of mine is the case of a friend's father who, hoping to run away from his forty-year marriage in Manchester, did just that and escaped to London and the arms of a pretty young nurse. His wife, after two months of waiting for him to return, took the train to London ... and there, two streets away from the station, walked straight into him. Well, you could say Jean Hastie's luck, on that Wednesday in February, was getting near to that kind of odds. For, within minutes of leaving the bus in Portobello Road, walking northwards, Jean had her first sighting of her prey.

There is probably as little need here to describe the streets where Eliza Jekyll's old friend Jean Hastie and her alarming new quarry Mrs Hyde were walking on that dreary afternoon as there is to transcribe Mrs Hastie's research on early Hebraic depictions of the Garden of Eden. Suffice it to say that most of the stall-holders in the market, deterred by the weather and the sparsely populated pavements, had gone home. A bread shop gave off the only warm glow, in the stretch of Portobello Road just before it ducks under the great bridge of Westway; and beyond that, by the second-hand and occult shops, a mean wind wafted nothing more satis-fying than paper bags and Smartie cartons to the sleep-ing homeless by the entrance to the Tube.

Something seemed to press Jean Hastie to go on. She is not the sort of person, as we have seen, who would admit to instinct or premonition as a guiding force; but her entry for Wednesday the eleventh does own to a kind of 'drivenness', making her walk, without know-ing (and almost as a foreigner to the city after all these years, and certainly a stranger in these remoter regions of North Kensington) her exact location or even compass direction as she went. Golborne Road, she says, was the last time she had any bearing on her position; yet something drew her always on, so that within five or ten minutes she was neither pleased nor concerned to find herself at the edge of a vigorously rippling brown canal.

This is where the extreme unlikeliness of Jean's prey appearing comes in. And yet it did, despite the distance from the part of Notting Hill where Mrs Hyde could reasonably be expected to be seen; and, more importantly perhaps, without the hunter knowing exactly why and how she looked there.

Imagine the scene . . . a turning down a crumbling street leads Jean Hastie to a bridge . . . a bridge with two pathways, as if those crossing over must return by the other way . . . and on the far side of the low, humped metal bridge, is a great red-brick warehouse, with words lit up in a neon glare in the surrounding winter gloom of water, asphalt and a grudging strip of towpath: CANALOT STUDIOS. There is no sound, apart from the ripple of water. Other warehouse fronts, grey and dingy yellow, stand by the studios and front a line of water that looks as thirsty for bodies as any French river in the age of suicides. Yet no one lurks, waiting for the moment to run out . . . only Jean Hastie stands there, on the bridge, looking down. For, outside the main doorway of the red-brick giant, a woman is rustling in a rubbish bin. You can't hear her, because of the water . . . and, too, because of a blast of rock music from the studios as the main door swings open and a group of polo-necked young men come out . . . and by the time they have crossed her path and the glimpse of the white-marbled fountain and palm-filled interior has faded again with the bobbing to of the door, it is too late. The canal is as empty and as dead as ever, the quick whispering of the water no more than an illusion of depth and changingness. On the far side of the warehouses, where Jean goes as she runs over the bridge to catch the woman, Harrow Road lies in a blur of TV shops and Chinese takeaways. And here, as if luck had come to Jean Hastie and was determined to stick to her for the rest of the day, walks Mrs Hyde in a street as rough and garish and abandoned to the poor as that great warehouse behind her is a haven for creativity and wealth.

It was clear that Mrs Hyde had some messages to get – as Jean Hastie puts it. She went into a cheap butcher, and out again with a bundle wrapped in paper so thin the mince oozed at the sides; she went to a shoe-mender's bar and emerged with two small pairs of shoes, not wrapped up at all and forced to share a dingy shopper with the mince. She went – suddenly – into a betting shop and there she stayed.

Jean Hastie had, as she recalls, two choices at this point. She could go into the bookie's after the woman; or she could go home by Ladbroke Grove (for she knew well enough where she was now, the stretch of water and old windowless buildings on the canal having temporarily dislocated her) and wait for her prey to come home. No one, Jean reckoned, would go much further on an evening like this, with mouths to feed and meat soaking through the lining of a bag. But choose she must; for she had been seen spying; and Mrs Hyde's wasn't the only head – in an area where to be quick is a matter of survival – to have turned with the speed of a key in a lock at the sight of Jean Hastie strolling down Harrow Road.

It soon became clear that the first option was out of the question. What was she to say to this woman, whom she had seen only once, after all, in the gardens and late at night? (It's odd here, as Jean remarks, that she was so sure the woman was Mrs Hyde: it had to do with the stooping run, the air of almost palpable disintegration and of course the infamous white mac, worn now over a nondescript skirt and sweater.) The very thought of stopping such a pathetic creature – or undeserving no-hoper, depending on how you saw these things – was repellent to the solicitor and mother of two. Besides, how could she question the woman while surrounded by punters intent on changing the course of their luck? All hell might break out. Despite her provincial manner, Jean Hastie knew enough of bad areas in inner cities to desist from plunging into the heart of a better's den.

In she went, though. She wasn't sure, as she records in her diary, what decided her, in the end: it was the possible frustration, very likely, of losing Mrs Hyde again; and of waiting, unrewarded, on a corner of Ladbroke Grove while her interviewee vanished from the face of the earth (not, as Jean told Robina Sandel when she came back scared and cold from her quest for Eliza Jekyll's beneficiary, that that, or something very like it, hadn't taken place in front of her own eyes when her quarry did finally make her way back to the dilapidated houses concealing gardens and richly stuccoed crescents behind). But at least she'd got some picture of her – and here Jean shuddered again and took the hot toddy proffered by Robina gratefully. We must regret this, for the rest of the entries for that afternoon's encounter are short and stumbling, dwindling to silence after only a paragraph or two.

Mrs Hyde, apparently, had won some money on a horse, McCubbin, the day before. (All this as related by Robina, as told her by Jean; and I think some of Robina's fanciful humour must have crept in here and there.) The woman was even joking that she'd spent the children's family allowances on the bet; and it must have been a well-worn joke, for the only person to look up, chortle, through a fag glued to lower lip, was a fat woman with some disease resembling porphyria, her purple double chins subsiding into one another as she laughed.

'Mrs Hyde?' Jean Hastie said.

A chatter of odds and races followed; the woman Jean had pursued with so much attention since hearing her old friend Eliza's commission, now looked away, turning up the collar of her sweater and pulling down her head under the mac so that for a moment she looked cowled, a medieval martyr, or a woman who has just been shriven and is being taken off to be burned. 'Can I see your face?' Jean Hastie asked.

The sound of the racing swelled, and the fat woman pushed forward. A man bumped up against Jean and obscured her from seeing anything other than synthetic tweed, ash-covered and drink-soaked from repeated efforts to lift a beer can in the jostling crowd.

And I did see her face, Jean told Robina. And I can't describe it at all. It had nothing to distinguish it.

Mrs Hyde had asked Jean Hastie why the hell she wanted to see her face. 'I thought she was going to kick me – or fly at me – then and there. But I kept my ground. The drunk was lurching his way out of the betting shop into the Harrow Road. The fat woman, like some mud wrestler – like those women in TV who are just rows of muscle under the fat – moved up to Mrs Hyde as if to protect her.'

'We have friends in common,' Jean said. 'Eliza Jekyll –' she added quickly, when the expressions on the faces of Mrs Hyde and her companion showed extreme disbelief that a woman in twinset and suit of a real tweed should have friends in common with such as these – not to mention the improbable venue of a bookie in one of the roughest streets in an already rough area, to decide to make a claim of social acquaintanceship.

'You mind your own fucking business,' said Mrs Hyde.

Jean Hastie, as she sipped her toddy – and took more without demur from Robina's big silver ladle – said Mrs Hyde had finally, after a good deal more abusive language, admitted to knowing Ms Jekyll – but not that they were friends. 'I suppose she realized this was all to do with the flat,' Jean said (for, after her unpleasant adventure, she felt the time had come to confide in her hostess). 'She didn't want to jeopardize her chances. What she didn't know,' the Scottish solicitor added with some feeling, 'is that it's over my dead body she gets that flat from Eliza. It's blackmail, you mark my words.'

The rest of the story concerns Jean's return to No. 19

Nightingale Crescent and the strange vision she suffered in the middle of the most congested stretch of Ladbroke Grove.

'I swear that woman has been "appearing" to me today,' Jean said. 'I mean, it's hardly possible that a human being can vanish from sight in front of your eyes – in swirling traffic – just dematerialize, like that!'

There was no possibility that Jean Hastie had been drinking before taking some of the punch, Robina said. She was stone-cold sober – so cold, in fact, that a hot-water bottle had been placed on her feet and a warm plaid on her knees. Robina liked her guests to feel at home.

'Yet there she was,' Jean said. 'And then – there she wasn't. I never saw her after leaving the betting shop. She could have flown home on a broomstick, for all I know. Then – just like that, the earth swallows her up –'

Robina had lit two fat candles this time and the rest of the comfortable, London-worn room was in shadow. A haze of light rose in the faces of the two women as they pondered, and drank the wine and brandy and cloves, helping themselves from a silver bowl where a thin blue flame ran in circles under the eyes of the two white wax sentinels above.

'Perhaps Mephistopheles finally came to claim her,' Robina said. And she laughed softly, as if for a time – for that evening, at least – the old tales of the Germans and the Scots might come together and be true.

Certainly, as Jean Hastie remembered, there had been a hellish aspect to the junction of Ladbroke Grove and the Crescent, as she returned from her unexpected –

almost dreamlike – visit to the canal and the betting shop beyond.

Most of the street seemed to be in the process of being dug up, for one thing. Yellow diggers and dumpers moved like giant crabs in a sludge of churned earth and mud, their feelers reaching higher than the uppermost windows of the houses. Lamp-posts, facsimiles of the Victorian originals and insisted on by rich residents of the borough as replacements for the fluorescence of past decades, stood marooned on their islands of concrete as the road-widening exercise took place. The demure light they afforded – particularly as even this was shrouded by protruding rhododendron and privet from front garden hedges – had made Jean apprehensive. She was glad, she told Mara as they sat on the morning after her adventure in Mara's upper bedroom at No. 19, to have rounded the corner from the Grove; but in the main thoroughfare, at least, the lights of the roadworks had been bright enough to see where you were going.

The odd thing, Mara said, was that Jean had clearly been very much shaken by the whole thing. 'It's unlike her. She's become – well, a lot more conservative since we used to see a lot of one another. We don't have much in common now, I suppose you could say. And she's working on some theory of Original Sin as perceived in the first four centuries after Christ, before St Augustine came along and made his own interpretation of St Paul – saying, in effect, that free will is only an illusion, that we are all saddled with Original Sin: "sin that dwells in me, because I was the son of Adam".'

I couldn't see what Jean's researches had to do with it, and I said so. What we are trying to do, after all, is to piece together the events both psychological and actual of the days in what the media opportunistically like to refer to as 'Valentine's Day', or Week; and a matter of prime importance, as it now appears, is the highly improbable vanishing of Mrs Hyde under the eyes of the busy visitor from Fife.

Jean had insisted, however, on sticking to her story. The lights from the mechanical diggers were flashing; a thin drizzle was falling; here and there, like the red eye of a dinosaur, the light at the top of a crane swung into view. The roadworks had caused an appalling traffic jam, and Jean threaded her way through cars and concrete mixers to reach the pavement as it rounded and went up the Crescent towards No. 19. It was then, Jean said, that she realized that the crumbling houses of Ladbroke Grove, made even more insecure now by the sudden absence of pavement in front of them, were connected with the stucco palaces behind. For an open door in one of the most dilapidated houses, combined with a flare of brightness from the magnesium torches in the street, showed a passageway – then another door open wide – and beyond that a window, which gave out on the black, rural peace of communal gardens. At the same time, a figure of a man dashed out of the house and down the steps and Mrs Hyde, now discernible on the cordoned-off fragment of walkway made available for pedestrians in this grand scheme, came nearer, walking down from the north end of Ladbroke Grove.

There were some things, Jean insisted, which would remain in her mind a long time – and the first was by no means the descent into the ground of her original prey. No, it was the sight of the two faces at the basement window – of the house with the open door from which the man was running – the house towards which Mrs Hyde had, to all intents and purposes, been making her way – two faces, behind grimy, once-white bars, that looked up and wrung Jean Hastie's heart so that she had, in turn, to stop in her tracks and look down.

It must have been then – so Jean supposes – that Mrs Hyde 'nipped off' somewhere else. For it is, after all, impossible to go down into the bowels of the earth in the middle of a busy street in London. Yet she could have sworn, when she looked up from her anguished contemplation of these children – so different from her own bairns: so pale and underfed and miserable, such examples of an upbringing in the cruel city – that she saw, just for one split second, the figure of Mrs Hyde, as she went down. 'I know it can't be,' Jean said as Mara – and then Robina Sandel, called upstairs to hear the tale one more time – questioned her again. The man had run off, up the Grove towards Notting Hill. Jean was clear on that. But where – and you had to think of those poor children at the window – where was their mother now?

* * *

Jean Hastie had more than a few thoughts to contend with, as she left Ladbroke Grove and walked away from the bulldozers and pickaxes, towards the haven of Robina Sandel's house. Here the leather club fender and the air of battered permanence so soothing to inmates and visitors in an age of rapid change, demolition and reconstruction, would at least be the same as when she left earlier that day; here, too, she could hope to find Dr

Frances Crane in a better frame of mind than before: prepared, possibly, to answer her urgent questions on Mrs Hyde and to allay some of her anxieties. She hurried on, uneasily aware that she, if not the ambience at No. 19, had certainly changed since her recent arrival. For how could it be, when she had passed nothing more alarming than a peeling house – the scaffolding proclaiming a return to mansion status; notices warning trespassers of dogs and prosecution; and then had walked right by a fine window, lit to show the terracotta hues of the room inside to the best advantage, with four or five people gathered in it, by a dark bookcase and guarded, as it seemed, by marble pilasters – that she felt, quite unequivocally, afraid? The lash of a shrub, wet and cold against her face, made her ashamed to admit that she would prefer the maelstrom of Ladbroke Grove to the sudden, suffocating silence of this residential place. Somewhere in the gardens, behind the tall houses that lean just visibly against each other in their shallow foundations, an owl hooted. And Jean Hastie, telling herself she must make some sense out of this whole puzzle, walked back past the tableau in the terracotta room, and at a greater speed past the sheeted and iron-girt No. 39. Next door was a flight of stone steps, and here Jean rang on a bell where was inscribed, under a transparent shield that was also discreetly lit from behind, the name E. JEKYLL.

'So you decided not to wait for Eliza's dinner party?' Mara Kaletsky said when Jean paused, as if trying to find words to convey what she had then seen. 'You were worried for her, right? How much you need to be I don't really know. But she seems the kind of woman who can look after herself – wouldn't you say?'

Jean said she had been worried all the same. If her old friend was actually being menaced by some kind of psychotic – well, she was in need of help and there was an end to it. If she was simply going through one of her foolish phases – then Jean would refuse absolutely to draw up any legal documents for her.

'I was let in by entryphone – actually it turns out to be video,' Jean said, with some of the naïvety of a countrywoman. 'A woman who was tidying up in there let me into Eliza's ground-floor flat. I must say, I was most impressed.'

Robina Sandel and Mara had difficulty in avoiding each other's glances at Jean's reverence for the décor installed by Eliza – a good deal more sophisticated, as Jean pointed out, than anything she would have expected of her at art school in Oxford. The front hall, Jean said, had been mirrored with old glass so that it was impossible to tell where it ended and the rest of the flat began; and when you did go through, ushered in by . . . who was it . . . Grace . . . ?

'Yes. Roger Poole the gardener's wife,' Robina said, impatient already with these eulogies for a lifestyle of which she could only disapprove. 'She cleans for people round the gardens – on occasions.'

'I was lucky, though.' Jean was breathless now with her description of the living room and its all-embracing mural, where every available surface was covered with what appeared to be ancient scenes. 'I was lucky, I mean, to be able to talk to Grace. Because she enabled me to feel that there is indeed something the matter with poor Eliza's life: that she is, certainly, in desperate need of some assistance; and that I am the one to help her – as no one else would be able to do.'

* * *

As is evident from Jean Hastie's journal, filled in the evening after her encounter with the elusive Mrs Hyde, an element of fear – of panic, almost – had begun to take root; and Jean's efforts to eradicate it and return to the world of St John Chrysostom are almost pathetic to read.

Her sense, I believe, of the 'closeness' of Mrs Hyde to Eliza Jekyll, gleaned from the meeting with Grace Poole in Eliza's empty apartment, had brought the subject with which she was concerned in her researches more close to her – for the journal, speculating on the nature of Original Sin and the irreconcilable split in each and all of us that came in the Garden of Eden, concludes that there is no hope for the human race unless we return to the position of the first Christians, viz., that we are indeed free and responsible for our actions.

No woman, however 'down on her luck', has the right to demand of another what Mrs Hyde was clearly extorting from her friend and neighbour. Neighbour! That was where the closeness came in, and it riled Jean Hastie to confess to the bad night she suffered after her visit to Ms Jekyll's flat. But confess, in the confidential pages of her diary, she did. The old clock tower at the top of St John's Gardens struck five before she found sleep. And when she woke, to a pale and watery morning, it was as if the sleep had been no more than a loan to her from the choked cemeteries of the past, so many strange and vivid figures did she see parading on exotic shores.

It would probably be easy to point out that the Pompeiian mural in Eliza's flat was responsible for these dreams of an alien world. At any rate, Jean transcribes, on waking and downing coffee brought her by Robina in her basement bedroom, the following exchange with Mrs Poole (and not before confiding that, ashamed as she is of blurting Eliza's request to the German householder, she had felt Mrs Sandel's hostility to her curiosity and now was confident that she would receive help in her inquiries on the vexed subject of Mrs Hyde).

Jean writes:

I couldn't help wondering, as I stood in that room of Eliza's – quite small, in reality, if you measured it, but so cunningly done up you could honestly feel you were in a Roman villa somewhere in the heart of the Calabrian countryside (and that in February!) whether Mrs Poole knew something of what was going on between the two women . . . two women who live so close, as I thought with a sinking of the heart, that it's very likely they can hear each other through the wall or, even, have a communicating door. Not for the first time, as I asked Grace Poole whether Eliza was expected to come back soon, I felt that this proximity must force me away from the whole matter. It is none of my business, after all. Yet the very thought of having a woman such as Mrs Hyde so appallingly close made me hesitate again, when it came to walking out of the door at Mrs Poole's civil reply.

'No, Eliza [that was how she called her] has been out some time, love.'

I weighed up Mrs Poole carefully before asking her the next question. She seems a homely type of woman, a bit sloppy in her habits perhaps, from the out-of-place pockets of untidiness in Eliza's beautiful room: a wad of tissues on a low table by the marbled wood fireplace, a sweet wrapper (of all things!) on the floor by the door to the hall. But she seems straightforward enough; and was straightforwardly disappointing, too, when she said she didn't 'do' this place more than once in a blue moon – 'but there's a dinner party tomorrow night and so she asked me to come in'. By the time I got round to asking about 'the other woman' (as I feel Mrs Hyde must be, in some way, in Eliza's sexual past – unless she's an ex-employee . . . or a member of the family who's in trouble? Hardly, no) Mrs Poole was, in the politest way possible, showing me to the door. There are ruched blinds in the flat, which give an even more cocooned feel to the place, and she flicked one up a foot or so to pull the window shut before turning off the light of the central chandelier and making to go after me.

'Mrs Hyde?' Grace Poole said as we stood a second in the darkened room, lit only by a beam of light from someone's house in the gardens. 'Oh yes, she has a key. Not that I've seen her here, mind you. She'll usually go in her entrance, out front.' Then, looking at me with a sudden interest: 'You a relative or something, dear? Come into town to see her, have you?'

[There was something about the whine of the London woman's voice, the obviousness of Jean's 'foreignness' in these parts and the discomfort of standing any longer in such artificial conditions that made Jean move abruptly to the window – in the opposite direction, of course, to the door to the hall and the way out. Mrs Poole made a tut-tutting sound behind her.]

I looked out of the window just revealed to me by Mrs Poole, [are Jean's last words in her entry for Wednesday the eleventh of February] and straight into the basement window of a littered pipe-clogged kitchen. The windows were filthy – and steamed over as well – but I could see who was standing at the sink, face partially obscured by one of those old Ascot water heaters they used to put in thirty or forty years ago. It was Mrs Hyde all right, and she was peeling tatties with a sharp, serrated knife that had a red handle; her hands were red too, and the water was spurting out scalding, as if she couldn't care less for the heat. The poor wee bairns were there, and now and again she'd shout at one or other of them. A black cat was on the kitchen table – if you could call a sagging strip of Formica with legs by such a name.

She looked up and straight at me. It was her bare bulb that lit Eliza's room.

Then I followed Mrs Poole back into the hall. And I nearly tripped over the umbrella stand, which I hadn't seen before! It just shows how these mirrors and trick paintings and that sort of fantabulasia can drive ye blind as a bat! Mrs Poole was quite irritated with me by now – and I with her, that I could be mistaken for a kinswoman of that monster across the way.

As I say, I tripped on Eliza's umbrella. A weird object: wood, with a parrot's head and a long, scarlet-painted beak.

I like a thing to be what it is, and no' pretend to be anything else – as my aunt Peggy used to say.

61

As it so happened, Thursday, the twelfth of February, dawned bright and clear, and stayed that way all day: so cold that birds sang and then stopped, on branches etched white with frost; but with a sun that everyone in London seemed to have forgotten, so that children skated shouting on frozen puddles and their women, mothers or minders, bent down for the first crocus or stretched for the egg-yolk yellow of forsythia against a wall.

The horrors of preceding days in the communal gardens of North Kensington seemed to have been blown away along with the bad weather. The great damp blanket of rain and cloud that had lain over the city with as much persistence as the Victorian fogs of the past, had brought with it the rustle of suspicion, the stifled tread in darkness of the murderer. It was true that the Notting Hill rapist had not yet been caught – but on a day like this, he hardly came to mind. The trees were so thin you could see through them. The shrubbery, so often a menace at night when, like a locked wardrobe, it threatened to contain all manner of forgotten and execrable forms, had an innocent sparkle on deep green leaves. Tonight, too, would be bright and clear, with as fine a setting of stars as the cut-crystal, silver and bone arrangements of Ms Eliza Jekyll's dining table. There would even be a full moon, to guide those of the guests who preferred to stroll on such a perfect winter evening along the path at the back of the houses, to Eliza's garden steps.

Jean Hastie was one of these. She was, as she confesses in her journal (after a long disquisition on the bravery and freedom of the fourth century St Perpetua at Carthage) more than slightly ashamed of the 'uncomfortable feeling' to which she had owned the day before. And, although she would be loath to say that the change in the weather had been at the root of a return to her optimistic and cheerful manner, there was little doubt that the transparency of the evening and the pretty twinkling lights from the prosperous houses of Nightingale Crescent, made her feel glad to be alive – and glad, too, that she had a delightful family to return to. Like the hysteria in the gardens over the prowler, the schism in the church after St Augustine – and the subject of his own overriding lust, cause of his theory of the inherited nature of man's sin – seemed far away to an ordinary, contented housewife such as Jean Hastie. She felt sorry, certainly, for those like Mara (who trotted beside her under a moon the size of a silver pomander, the inevitable video camera slung round her neck) and their tiny, claustrophobic view of the world. All London was there, after all, for the sampling (Jean had, after a successful day in the British Library, stopped off at the National Gallery and seen the Impressionists on loan from Moscow and Leningrad). Only, as Jean dourly remarked to herself, it seemed that some women couldn't see it like that.

The women here, living as they did with a dangerous attacker in their midst, could think of little else – and their own position as women in regard to him and other men, of course. It is stultifying, Jean confides to her diary just before going to bed later that night, to find human beings restricted precisely by their need to redefine themselves, to find 'freedom'. And she swears, once this book is done, that she will take a long break from the subject and enjoy life in Fife without a further thought for Eve – or the serpent, for that matter. 'W–O–M–A–N', she says with determination, 'is a word which will be erased from my typewriter.'

It wasn't surprising that the picture of a silver pomander comes up, when we hear that the enticing smell of Eliza Jekyll's cinnamon and clove punch wafted down almost as far as the back garden of No. 19 – and was certainly in evidence as Jean and Mara, at peace with each other tonight, strolled on a path icing-white by the side of dark, churned earth prepared for spring planting. Jean said something to the effect that she'd better be careful with the toddy this time around; and Mara, laughing, agreed: as if all the hobgoblins summoned that night at Robina Sandel's had lain in a bottle of house red warmed with a scrap of West Indian spices and a floating slice of orange. But, with all the back curtains of the residents' magnificent sitting rooms drawn back – as if on a night like this, with such a high, vaulted sky and a pantomine moon, it would be criminal to shut it behind the chintzy curtains – it was little wonder that there was a feeling of benign, neighbourhood watch: a truly communal spirit in the air.

Jean saw the family she had passed on her visit to Eliza by the Crescent way – sitting still in their front bay window but visible from behind, like going into the back of the Pollock's toy theatre she had had as a child. They were listening to music – Mozart, Jean recognized – and didn't hear the scrunch of her and Mara's shoes on the pebble path. But Mara waved to them all the same. 'Jeremy Toller and his dear ones,' she said, surprising Jean with the bitterness and dislike in her voice. 'They've done *nothing* to help catch the rapist. And Toller's a local magistrate!'

Before there was time for Jean to drop the hint – something she had been longing to do all day, when it came to explaining to Mara that there was more to the world than just this garden, threatened though it might be by evil – the two old friends had come to Eliza's steps and were beginning to go up them. Neat flowerbeds, arranged in a radial petal design, lay to their left – the Tollers' garden, presumably, and tended with extreme care and forethought, some of the shrubs tied, staked and protected from the winter winds by loving hands. To their right, as Jean saw with a pang of dismay, was a very different story. And, as Mara made no comment on the contrast between the two plots of land, Jean Hastie decided to look straight ahead and arrive on Eliza Jekyll's terrace in a fit mood for an enjoyable dinner party.

It was hard, however, not to look down one more time before they stood outside the curtained french window at the back of Eliza Jekyll's drawing room and tapped (a prearranged signal) to be let in. For there was something almost 'surreal – if that's the word', as Jean wrote later, before the further events of the night became known to her. A rotting pianola, reminiscent indeed of some Buñuelesque fantasy, lay in the garden adjacent to Eliza Jekyll's, its gashed keyboard and rotting marquetry long ago eaten away by rain and frost and squatted by passing cats. The garden, if so it could be called, seemed to have grown humpy, under a patchy covering of grass, as if a mass of botched graves had been attempted there; and under the window that looked out on all this lay, like a child's stick drawing of a man thrown sideways, the white rails of a broken plastic clothes horse. The light in the window was off, but Jean recognized only too well the chipped wooden sills and flaking cream paint of Mrs Hyde's kitchen. And it was with an even greater sense of resolution that she walked in through heavy, textile curtains to Eliza's painted room of trick colonnades and marble antechambers, among which her guests stood waiting to be introduced. She would relax as far as was possible during dinner, Jean told herself with her customary firmness. But she would have an equally firm word with Ms Eliza Jekyll before the night was out.

*   *   *

MARA'S FILM

Mara, proud of her 'docudrama', says that without her ever-present Video 8 camera we'd have no idea of the talk or mood of the dinner in the flat that night; and that this is true is borne out by the abrupt cessation of Jean Hastie's journal after she returned to No. 19. Her last recorded thoughts are on the beauty of the winter evening and the distressing mess of the garden that lies between the fine houses of Nightingale Crescent and the back of Ladbroke Grove, making a sort of a squalid courtyard between the two. So – Jean breaks off here, which is the greatest pity, as far as our investigations are concerned – and, for this evening at least, Mara takes over.

The sound on her loaned camera is working this time, and after the regulation tour of the table (gravadlax with dill sauce on mother-of-pearlized plates, French bread piping hot, fine china and slender white candles in silver candlesticks) we see first the hired help as he comes out of the tiny kitchenette at the side of Eliza's elegant room. 'That's what they do these days, the high-fliers,' Mara says as we watch the man in a spotless tuxedo unload stores in the mirrored hall. 'They get the whole thing sent round, staff and all, on a credit card!'

The guests, as Mara then points out gleefully, could have come as some package offer as well. Sir James Lister, proprietor of the Shade Gallery and much else, looks, in his smoking jacket of plum velvet with satin facings, like an ad on TV for port or some expensive liqueur. Lady Lister, in black beaded chiffon and lace, with hair as thin spun as the strawberry meringue the hired help is at this moment unpacking from a hamper, looks as if she were herself advertising a marriage bureau of the more discreet type. Then, in trousers and leather jerkin and bottle-green dress respectively, Monica Purves and Carol Hill come into focus. A small, almost hairless man – an art critic, Mara explains – is next. They all stand near the table, for the room, despite its painted avenues, is very small; and then with a maddening deliberation that Mara speeds up for fun, they sit down.

Yes, it does seem that Eliza wants to talk to her friend Jean Hastie. She has Sir James Lister on the other side, it's true – and we hear on a loud and sighing soundtrack the tycoon's proposition that Eliza should meet him for a 'Valentine Day lunch in that little place in Holland Park Avenue?' and see her frown and then smile and agree. But it's to Jean she turns – as soon as the marinated salmon has been cleared away and magret de canard, with its exotic bilberry and cardamom sauces has been served – and it's on her face that Mara now trains her lens, so that she is in close-up, like stars in the movies used to be: Ingrid Bergman in *Casablanca* perhaps: appealing, mysterious.

Maybe one makes that comparison because Eliza Jekyll is not only looking quite outstandingly beautiful tonight, but young and – with which even Mara has to agree – surprisingly soft and vulnerable. 'High-flier' she may be, but butter wouldn't melt in her mouth. Mara would say that this is because the butter, along with every other damn thing, is brought to the door, care of American Express. (Which means, she adds, c/o Sir James Lister, who is perfectly clearly paying for all this.) 'Look,' Mara says as the camera hovers low and shows Sir James's hand on Eliza's knee. 'And look at Lady Lister's face. She's none too pleased, if you ask me!'

Despite the booming conversation conducted by Monica Purves and the art critic on the subject of *glasnost* and the future of Soviet art, it is possible to hear Jean Hastie and Eliza talk; and if Mara cannot at times resist changing the camera angles in a fanciful way, it's still possible to get the gist of what they're saying.

JEAN: Tell me, Eliza, don't you think you should reconsider? I may tell you that I feel quite worried on your behalf.

ELIZA: (*As camera pans to a Pompeiian panel of her room, this in turn replaced by a close-up of the hired butler's hands as he offers a dish of mange-touts and tiny new potatoes*) My dear Jean, I only ask you to ask as few questions as

68

you can. You don't know how much I need and depend on that woman. I think of her very highly indeed. I owe her, you might say, almost everything.

Here we are shown the look of amazement on Jean Hastie's face. She must ask further – she has seen this unworthy recipient of Eliza Jekyll's charity in a light which, surely, Eliza should be told about: she mentions the visit to the betting shop, the children's allowances gambled away. Eliza, misty-eyed, shakes her head. She knows it looks bad . . . but doesn't Jean herself speak and act as she does now from feelings of an old loyalty? Imagine – so much this woman needs – life's impossible in London now, for the poor, the single mother – how can Jean Hastie refuse to help her?

She shall have the flat, Eliza says, and as she speaks she flinches away from the pressure of the hand under the table – looking, as she does so, like a bird caught in a net, fluttering, beseeching on either side. ('They all look like that,' Mara says. 'It's the post-feminist trick. Using the wiles of Marilyn Monroe to achieve the aims of Stalin.')

JEAN: But one more time, Eliza. If we make over this place to – to your friend . . .

ELIZA: Mrs Hyde. Without her I would be lost, I assure you, Jean . . .

JEAN: And if something should happen to you, Eliza? Where would you go then?

ELIZA: (*Confused suddenly*) Happen to me, Jean? What do you mean?

It must be said that a kind of basic decency in Jean Hastie does make itself discernible here. Worried, no doubt, by the kind of translucent quality Eliza seemed to project that evening ('She was like – I can't describe it – something like the sky at home before a storm,' Jean told Robina Sandel) the Scots solicitor decided against pressing her case any further. Suggestions that a London conveyancing firm would be more suitable than herself for the drawing up of a lease brought only a violent shake of the head and something very like tears forming in exquisitely made-up eyes. Jean, by the time the meringue and compôte of Caribbean fruits have arrived, has agreed to Ms Eliza Jekyll's request. And conversation becomes general, with property prices (an indignant Monica Purves) and a sale in Somerset of netsuke daggers (Sir James) which he and his wife will visit the next day, taking precedence as topics on this occasion over the Notting Hill rapist. No doubt this is because Mara Kaletsky, wandering out into the hall to get a long shot of the dinner table, has found a door among the panels of age-stained Venetian glass and opened it to go through.

* * *

WHAT TILDA SAW

Robina Sandel tells me it took her niece some time to shake her awake, the morning of the murder.

It was the thirteenth of February – 'Friday the thirteenth', as Robina says with that wry smile which both discounts and accepts old superstitions. She'd been dreaming – tropical birds and jungles, the dream had been. Maybe it reflected the terror that stalked them each night, she said, ready to pounce like a wild beast through carelessly open window, or ventilation shaft: maybe, again, the brightly coloured birds she saw were

70

prophetic, omens of the bloody murder to come. For Tilda was sure of one thing, when her aunt was finally propped up on a pillow, eyes wide open with the shock of Tilda's screams. It was a parrot that had killed the man – deep into his throat, with its beak.

It took some time to make sense of Tilda's story. She was sleeping upstairs now – and sleeping better than she had been when down in the basement, with the door straight out to the shrubbery Robina never got round to trimming. She, unlike her aunt, had dreamed of war; and this time there was no need for magical beliefs to trace the origins of the dream. Twice she had woken and heard the very real sound of a police helicopter overhead. Perhaps because she felt safe in the attic she'd dozed off again without much difficulty. Everyone knew the sound was a sign of another ineffective hunt for the rapist (some said he must be a member of the police force, to evade them so often) and yet, at an unconscious level, Tilda didn't care enough to wake up or go downstairs. It was something else that had woken her finally – and she and Robina had to laugh later about 'ze birds', as Mrs Sandel termed the nocturnal visitants to her and her niece's sleep that night – it had been the cry of an owl.

Tilda got up and went over to the mansard window in her tiny, sloping-walled room. She felt cold all over, she said: was it because the owl's hooting had come after the sound of the chopper had died away, thus showing the criminal uncaught and triumphant? Or was it, as the gullible Tilda was only too prone to believe, because the 'bad karma' of that evil woman Mrs Hyde in the gardens had floated up to her in her perch above the trees and told her of the approaching crime? Poor Tilda, whichever way it was, she was the last person who should be subjected to witnessing such a scene.

Mrs Hyde was visible – when Tilda had crawled out on to the ledge by her window and looked down – because something had set off the electronic security light in the Tollers' garden, several doors down.

She caught the man round the neck with her left arm. She'd come up behind him, as if she were about to overtake and wham! she'd hooked him with the left while the right brought this instrument down on the man's head. The spotlight had shown up, in its unblinking white light, the blood of the man as it spurted on the grass by the side of the path.

And the instrument – Tilda was sure of this because the scarlet paint of the beak had shown up strong in the beam – was one of those umbrellas you can get in the posh shops by Mr Christian's delicatessen at the end of the Crescent where it meets Portobello Road. An umbrella with a long, elegant handle and a parrot's head.

* * *

TWO LETTERS

Jean Hastie took the train north later that day. She was too shaken, she told Robina Sandel, to stay on at No. 19. She wanted to see her husband and children.

The atmosphere of jubilation in the gardens was more than she could stomach, too. 'I suppose I can just about understand,' she wrote to Mara, once safely ensconced in the noon express to Waverley, with tray-table, pen and a folder of notes on the Gnostic Gospels arranged in front of her. 'If you've been at the mercy of this man for so long you must feel some sense of overriding relief that he won't trouble you any more. But surely a murder is still the taking of the life of a human being? And it frightens me that you – and those such as Monica Purves – don't seem to consider men to belong to the human race any more. This can never be the route to a saner world. And remember: it is always a case of freedom of choice. None of us (other than the criminally defective) lacks the opportunity to refuse evil. As you will discover, important new knowledge on the origins of sin and the thinking of early Christians is coming to light. The message of the story of Adam and Eve in the Garden of Eden is that we are responsible for the choices we freely make, good or evil, just as Adam was.

Mrs Hyde is a killer and must be punished for her crime.

You speak of compassion for such as she. But she is where she is as a result of choices freely made by none other than herself.

Mara, I won't go on preaching at you. I want to tell you how pleased I was to see you again. But then of course this whole thing came along and overshadowed our reunion – my work – everything.

And now I must tell you of my last, hurried meeting with Eliza before I went off to catch the train.

I felt more and more apprehensive, as you might well imagine, at the contract Eliza had requested for transfer of her apartment to Mrs Hyde.

After the appalling and violent murder in the early hours of this morning, I knew one thing at least: that neither heaven nor hell would move me to do this "favour" for her now. And I decided to go along there and tell her, face to face.

Mara, I myself feel a great sense of relief.

If one good thing has come out of this lawlessness, it is the end of the relationship between Eliza Jekyll and Mrs Hyde.

Eliza came to the door in a lovely frothy pink *peignoir*. She'd obviously been asleep and looked a little haggard, I thought, but still perfectly beautiful – in a way, quite honestly, that I don't remember in her young days at the Ruskin. She had been warned earlier, she said, by the doorbell ringing and ringing, so she knew something must be wrong, but by the time she'd reached the front door, all she saw was the back of Roger Poole as he went at speed up Ladbroke Grove. "I called him," Eliza said, "but with all that din from the roadworks, he couldn't hear me."

It had been Mrs Toller who told her of the crime.

By that time there were policemen pouring into the gardens and a TV camera crew had tried to push their way in through her flat. "I told them to use the gate in Ladbroke Grove," Eliza said. She'd been quite annoyed by the intrusion, I could see.

"They tried next door?" I said – I don't know why.

Eliza flushed. Now she was getting really angry. "They think they can walk in anywhere, these people." Then suddenly she burst into tears and came to put her arm round me. "Oh, Jean," Eliza said. "I was such a fool, to allow that woman to trick me. Please forgive me for wasting your valuable time!"

I must say, I was only too pleased to hear all this, but I pretended to be very severe. "Eliza," I said, "can you give me your word that you'll never have anything further to do with Mrs Hyde?"

A sort of convulsion seemed to run through poor Eliza – I really can't describe it, except to say I suppose it's the first time I've seen a shudder like that. It was, truthfully, like witnessing someone meeting death coming towards them – and what's so terrible, they say, is that you see yourself walking towards you before you die. It was as if she was fighting something, Mara – she didn't turn round again (for now she'd gone to stand by her french window looking out on the garden in the gloom – so unlike yesterday!) but she said, in a low altered voice: "I've had a letter from her, Jean. I'll never see her again. Look, here!"

She held the letter out behind her back. She was ashamed that I should see her crying, I suppose. And I must confess I'm not too good with over-emotional women. I went and took it.

Eliza asked me to leave, and read it at home. By which she meant Robina's, no doubt – but I just didn't have the heart to tell her that I was really going home, in under an hour. So I took the letter and left.

Oh, Mara, this is a frightful thing.

I was so relieved at first, when I sat for just a wee minute to read the letter, on Robina's fender in the club room. It's written in a childish hand, like someone who's barely learned to write or read. And it uses childish language, too, when it thanks Eliza Jekyll for all the kindness she has shown – quite honestly I wouldn't have been surprised if it had gone on to say "thank you for having me", like children are taught to write when they've been to a party! But then she went on to say that

75

she knew she had done something wicked. That she must run. And that she would be safe, for she was going far away to a place where she would never be discovered. Nor would she ever "trouble" Eliza again – I was reminded of the language of an old-fashioned servant, just as much as a child.

I admit that, although I was sorry that Mrs Hyde might never be brought to justice, I was too happy that Eliza should be removed from her influence to care over much about it. Whatever Eliza had done in her youth, she surely didn't deserve as heavy a yoke as this woman round her neck for the rest of her life.

Robina Sandel came in and I showed her the letter.

She in turn told me about the murder weapon.

My blood runs cold as I write this. Thank God we have now crossed the border and are home. But the Christmas trees they have planted on the hills make me think of Germany – and of Robina's distinctly unpleasant laugh when she handed me back Eliza's letter.

Robina, working for the Resistance, became an expert on calligraphy. And just as much as the umbrella with the parrot's head is Eliza's – I remember it in the hall of her flat when I went looking for her that day – so is the letter from Mrs Hyde no more than a disguised form of Eliza's writing, writing known to Robina, who received a letter from her regarding a garden committee decision only the other day.

What has that wretched girl got herself into?

She must be deeper in with Mrs Hyde than ever before. Did she know her umbrella had been taken quite coolly from the hall, to commit the murder?

Presumably. In which case she is doing her best to cover up for Mrs Hyde, who has killed a man and must answer for the crime.

We've crossed the border now and soon I'll be home.

When I've finished my book on the origins of sin I shall work on the Enlightenment in Edinburgh, that most wonderful of cities; and I shall study the works of Henry Cockburn, the judge whose happiness came from a childhood in these hills.

It's dark already, and I want light.'

* * *

PART TWO

A VISIT TO JEAN HASTIE

It is August, and half a year has passed since the scandalous killing of a man in the communal gardens in what *Newsweek* referred to as 'West London's Yuppie Paradise'.

In the six months since the crime, there have been no less than 230 sightings of Mrs Hyde, from as far afield as Rio de Janeiro and Reykjavik, and – more frequently – Dieppe and the Costa Brava. Descriptions of the case as an inverted Lord Lucan are inevitable – or so the tabloids claim, painting a picture of the 'murderess' as a wronged woman, somewhere between an abandoned mistress and an underpaid drudge, who wrought her revenge on a member of the aristocracy.

For the victim was none other than Jeremy Toller, younger brother of Lord Pilsdon. A businessman, local magistrate and connoisseur of fine arts, Toller was soon removed from any suspicion of having been the Notting Hill rapist by the simple fact of the rapist's arrest while breaking in and attacking the landscape gardener Carol Hill only a few days after Toller was found dead.

Such an outbreak of violence in the gardens brought, not surprisingly, a flood of reporters and grisly crime-fans, eager to relish the atmosphere of the well-kept private park where a woman had battered a man to death. Some of these made their way to Robina Sandel's house at No. 19 Nightingale Crescent – and, in the case of the more wily and unscrupulous among them, they dressed up as Austrians, 'old friends' of Tilda's anxious to see her on their visit to London.

Robina, however, kept all callers at bay. And Mara Kaletsky left the country on the day after the crime – too deeply shocked, it was rumoured, by the reality of Mrs Hyde's act (though championing her cause energetically in the days before it took place) to stay in the neighbourhood. And there was another reason, as became clear when it was finally possible to glean information on those confusing days round the time of the murder: on February the fourteenth, quite unexpectedly, Sir James Lister closed down the Shade Gallery and announced plans to develop the site as a club/restaurant, with multi-level cinema and health facilities. Mara had, after all her work and preparation, lost her exhibition and suffered damage to her reputation as a painter and photographer. But that, as Robina Sandel commented grimly, is what England has now become – a 'quick-change artist', is the expression she used, I think, meaning that everything this country had once represented is liable overnight to be turned into its opposite.

Apart from Robina's further comments on the recognizable tide of Fascism she saw engulfing us all, there is little else of importance concerning events on the gardens, their precursors and consequences. This is partly because Jean Hastie's brief return to London in May did not take her to Robina Sandel's but to the Bay Hotel in Westbourne Grove. As Mara was abroad, there was probably little to persuade her to revisit the scene of the tragedy. Jean's fleeting visit and return to Scotland have dictated, however, my own journey north, to see Mrs Hastie and obtain from her, if possible, an account of those days in May. Her information, unless it consists exclusively of researches concluded at the British Library, can hardly fail to shed some light on the sudden decline of Dr Frances Crane.

I leave for Fife tomorrow, August the twelfth. Six months to the day, indeed, since the killing of The Honourable Jeremy Toller by Mrs Hyde.

I should have guessed, on the 'Glorious Twelfth', that a good housewife and mother such as Jean Hastie would be out on the moors with sandwiches and flasks of soup for the guns – that is, those like her husband and other worthies of the neighbourhood whose one desire is to return with a brace of grouse for the larder. I hadn't counted on the fact of Jean Hastie's being one such herself; and I must say it came as something of a shock, after reading all the morbid details of the Notting Hill case, to find her – I'd been directed from their farmhouse to a heatherclad stretch of hill, where estate wagons and Land Rovers could be seen, parked by a ruined cottage and a small burn – looking straight down the barrel of a gun at me.

That the shoot in progress was elsewhere was Jean Hastie's first assurance; less reassuring, I thought, was her statement that she hadn't seen me coming up the hill (though I'd been only too painfully aware of the foolishness of leaving my hired Ford Sierra at the bottom and tackling a steep ascent, even causing shouts of annoyance as I put up some birds), and the succession of thoughts that then came to me, I must admit, were quite a bit to do with the likely veracity of a witness who is both shortsighted and – presumably – hard of hearing. Ask I did, all the same, first introducing myself as a friend of Dr Frances Crane; and soon I was settled in the heather next to Mrs Hastie's picnicking site. While waiting for the next drive, she told me what she remembered of the days she had spent in London in May.

'Yes, it's a terrible thing,' Jean Hastie said. A cloud of pollen rose around us as I settled myself and I saw her for a moment through a brownish haze: she looked like a woman in an old sepia photograph, distinctly Victorian then, or so I thought; and I wondered if I would ever get the whole truth from her. She could easily, for reasons of discretion, hold something vital back: she could, I reflected with some irritation, have long ago decided to see life permanently through a sweet-scented, enveloping haze.

'I certainly did go and see Frances.' Jean offered me a drink of home-made lemonade from a stoppered bottle. 'I knew we were destined to become friends – as soon as we met at Robina Sandel's in February. It was the tension, I suppose, in the atmosphere then, that stopped us hitting it off immediately.'

'The tension caused by the rapist being at large?' I asked.

'Certainly. In my view some people had got the whole thing out of proportion.' Jean Hastie sighed, as if she alone were in possession of the secret of the important things in life, the threat to life itself – or, at the very least, to self-confidence – posed by an attack from a multiple rapist not being one of them. 'Mara Kaletsky for one. I honestly don't believe that an innocent man would have been killed if she and her – her friends hadn't incited that terrible woman to acts of violence. She'd already tried it once before, you know.'

'Who? You mean Mrs Hyde?'

'Yes. Mara told me she'd gone for Sir James Lister. He was walking down the street – to the corner of Ladbroke Grove, I think she said – and Mrs Hyde came charging at him and nearly broke his leg. With a wheeled shopper, or so Mara said.'

'Really?' I was beginning to see the vanishing murderer of Jeremy Toller in a new light; but what it was I couldn't at that moment quite tell.

'At least she's gone for good.' It was evident that Jean had pursued her quarry with the same tenacity her journals were to show. It occurred to me, slightly uncomfortably, that evil women like Mrs Hyde have a fascination for women such as Jean Hastie: as if a whole buried side to their nature, coming alive for a moment or so at the mention of the crime or whichever wicked deed, stirs pleasurably in them before subsiding again. It may account for the gigantic popularity of murder mysteries in England, I thought, and their huge female readership – for all the 'liberation' of the past couple of decades. And as for Scotland . . . we weren't far, it occurred to me, on this lonely hill, from the scene of many murders in border keeps . . . and tales, too of *doppelgängers* and people metamorphosed to beasts or three-legged stools, somewhere in the depths of the woods.

'What *is* good about the whole thing,' Jean Hastie said, 'despite the infuriating slowness of the police in catching Mrs Hyde, is the marked improvement in Eliza

Jekyll since the terrible woman has stopped battening on her. Yes, we all had dinner together – at her place – in May; and the other good thing is that Frances Crane was there. They'd fallen out over something, apparently – at least, in February they clearly weren't on speaking terms – yet in May, the seventh, I think it was, they were getting on like a house on fire. Monica Purves was there, too.'

'And Frances Crane seemed perfectly well then?' I said.

'Oh yes.' Jean Hastie shook her head in disbelief. A shout went up and a group of beaters appeared, signalling that the guns should return to their butts. Jean rose. I asked if I could go with her.

'Ye'll have to keep very quiet.' A schoolmistressy tone was employed to deliver this, and a markedly Scottish accent. I began to wonder if Mrs Hastie considered Frances Crane's misfortune to be mostly of her own making. Yet I was all the more determined to discover what Jean – possibly the last person to see her sane – had picked up in their final meeting.

The dinner had been so pleasant, Jean said, that she decided to forfeit a morning at the British Library and go and call on Dr Crane instead. She went first to the practice, in Walmer Road, where one of the two partners, Dr Bassett, said Dr Crane hadn't come in or phoned yet – and that this, while being most inconvenient for a line of waiting patients, was also most unusual. 'Then I went to her flat,' Jean said. 'No answer when I rang the bell. Of course I thought nothing of it. In fact I was quite glad to get back to the Library.'

This was the pattern of events on the eighth, ninth

and tenth of May. Once the front door had been opened by a woman who said she came in to clean twice a week and that Dr Crane wanted to see no one. On the eleventh of May (and here, I must say, I had to feel grateful for Mrs Hastie's perseverance) at seven in the evening, Jean stopped in Rudyard Crescent on the way back from completing her researches and banged once more on the door.

'The shock,' Jean said. 'I'll never be able to forget it.' We were crossing the burn on a small ford of flattish stones as she spoke, and for a moment Mrs Hastie looked as if she were going to lose her footing. Instead, with nothing worse than a wet brogue to contend with, she pulled herself up on the bank, where sheep's pellets lay thick in grass entwined, at the water's edge, with wild nasturtiums. Out of breath, we panted on to the summit of the first hill, where the men had already taken up their positions in shallow dug-outs in the heather.

'She looked, literally, forty years older!' There was something eerie about the way Jean Hastie spoke, as if the memory had indeed been of seeing a ghost. The breathlessness added to the sudden, shaming sense of panic which seemed to have overtaken us both, on this calm hillside with nothing but the curlew swooping over harebells and ling.

'She was . . . well, she was obviously dying,' Jean said in a matter-of-fact tone that belied her real feelings. 'She couldn't speak. She was white – and lined – and her hair – I suppose it must have been dyed or something and I'd never noticed it was growing out at the roots – was half-way grey so she looked – well, she didn't look like herself at all!'

I didn't know what to say at this point. We watched a flight of birds go over and heard a volley of shots, but Jean didn't so much as put her gun to her shoulder. When she did resume her tale, it was only to describe her terrified rush to Robina Sandel's – 'and thank God the woman was in' – and a phone call to Dr Crane's partner and then to the hospital.

'They – they came and took her away,' Jean said, 'with Robina and myself there to try and help her. But she wouldn't let us near her, you know. She was like a wild cat, hissing and scratching when we tried to come close. It took two ambulance men and Dr Bassett to pacify her. But – in the end – she went.'

I couldn't help shuddering myself. But I suppose Jean Hastie must have recovered quite a bit since then. It was four months ago, after all, and she had never known Dr Frances Crane well. It seemed, as she returned to telling me about the delightful summer party Ms Jekyll had given on that evening just a few days before the collapse of Dr Crane, that she was definitely more interested in the 'pink candlesticks on the chestnut trees – about a month ahead of the time they come out up here, I can tell you' and the real candles in art nouveau candlesticks that had adorned Eliza's table – than in the mysterious and horrible fate of the doctor. Maybe she's not so callous as she seems, I told myself as I saw Mrs Hastie, now fully composed after her tale, swing the heavy twelve-bore sky high and bring a bird whacking to the ground. Or, even if she is, this is no moment to antagonize her.

So I tried my most deferential manner, while

congratulating her on being an excellent shot; and then just happening to ask if Dr Crane had been able to communicate anything at all to her new-found friend.

'Yes, indeed.' Jean Hastie reloaded with care and deliberation. 'She handed me an envelope.'

'An envelope?' I felt like the stooge in a comedy turn. And, I reflected, there would be nothing to laugh about if only I could extract this envelope from Jean Hastie and take it to London with me.

'I'm here on behalf of Frances Crane's family and friends,' I said. 'It comes as a very great relief to learn that you have some kind of a document which will clear this extraordinary matter up. Their gratitude, I can assure you . . .'

Again, I felt my words drying up. Jean was waving to a plus-foured man, her husband, presumably, who was strolling down through the hummocks of moss and heather towards us. The drive was over, then; and this was soon borne out by a posse of beaters appearing from over the top of the hill.

'I'm afraid it's out of the question for me to show it to you,' Jean Hastie said. 'Nor have I been apprised of the contents myself, I may say.'

'You haven't . . .'

This time the husband (as indeed he was) had come near enough to call out a greeting and obscure my stumbling incomprehension following a repeated request to look at the material.

'Written on the envelope,' said Jean Hastie with a cool, almost contemptuous glance over her shoulder at me, 'are the words "Not to be Opened Unless the Disappearance of Ms Eliza Jekyll makes this Imperative". I have, of course, complied with Dr Crane's wishes in this matter.'

'But why should Eliza Jekyll want to disappear?' I cried. A pitch of frustration had been reached, I knew, which would reflect badly on me with these cool, canny Scots. And sure enough, Paul Hastie and his wife exchanged quick glances. 'Those are the instructions,' Jean said quietly. 'I represent Ms Jekyll – at least I was about to until such time as, happily, she no longer required me to perform a certain conveyancing service for her – and I shall of course guard her privacy as her friend Frances Crane would have wished.'

'But where *is* the . . . paper?' I faltered.

'From the size and weight of the envelope it would seem to be a cassette,' Mrs Hastie said, with some return of conviviality. 'And it is, of course, in the safe in my firm's office in Edinburgh.'

* * *

A WINDOW IN LONDON

August is dry and lifeless, with most of the residents of Nightingale and other Crescents in the area away in Scotland – or Italy or Greece. They won't return until the school terms begin and the leaves on the chestnut trees in the communal gardens begin to go yellow and fall.

I am disappointed, I must confess, by my lack of success so far with information on Dr Frances Crane. Robina Sandel, who kindly asked me to visit her at No. 19 Nightingale Crescent pending my researches, has this to say on the matter: 'Mrs Jean Hastie is a stubborn one, and she'll never let you have the tape.

Why don't you go and see Eliza Jekyll yourself and confide in her? For all you know, this is some trick being played on her by Jean Hastie – some kind of revenge, perhaps, from student days – and she'll be able to clear the whole matter up.'

I didn't relish the idea of going to call on Eliza Jekyll on my own and I said so. After all, we'd never met: surely she'd think it pretty out of order if I just went and banged on her door?

'Well, she's a friendly enough sort,' Robina said. 'Mara's coming back next Thursday, but no doubt you don't want to wait till then.' And seeing I didn't, she called her niece Tilda to walk down the street with me and introduce me to Ms Jekyll. Tilda had gone to help there with dinner parties in the past, Robina said; and although the girl had a horror of that end of the street, and particularly the garden side where she had witnessed Mr Toller's murder, she would understand my concern over my old friend Dr Frances Crane and would take me along. I thanked both Sandels for their kindness and understanding and Tilda and I set off.

Although it was only a week ago that we walked side by side down the Crescent, under heavy late-summer leaves and by the side of the now-silent road repair machines, it seems immeasurably longer – as if what was revealed to me in that time had a duration of its own, like a play, or a film – and could only exist in the memory by assuming quite different proportions. For though there seemed, on that tired August evening, to be no beginning, middle or end to the strange story of the murder in the gardens and the subsequent disappearance of Mrs Hyde and madness of Dr Frances

Crane, all these components came neatly together in the days succeeding my walk with Tilda, like a spool on a tape unwinding – like the voices of two women as I was to hear them before long, speaking not to each other but into the air.

Tilda, like a horse shying away from a sudden noise, stopped all at once outside a door and refused to go on, her pale eyes and braided hair giving her the look of a lifesize German doll that someone has left propped up on the pavement. Then, with a rush and a bound, as if spirits guarded that stretch, she raced ahead; and it was as much as I could do to keep up with her.

'But, Tilda, you've gone past Eliza Jekyll's door,' I said when I managed to catch up with the girl on the corner of Ladbroke Grove; and then, having to sprint again as she ran to the gate into the communal gardens and took out a key which she fitted quickly into the lock. 'Wait a minute, that's not right, Tilda. You're going to the wrong place!'

Tilda showed no sign of answering, and was by now some way down the path on the southern side of the communal gardens, the flat, dark leaves of the big chestnut at the back of the Tollers' house almost obscuring her head as she went. If she wanted to take me out here, why didn't she go out of Robina's back garden? I thought – irritated by now, I must admit, at the air of urgency and secrecy the girl had assumed. If she's trying to tell me something, why doesn't she do so in the ordinary way?

The answer, as I now see, was plain – to Tilda, at least. She did want me to see with my own eyes – see the connection of the houses on Ladbroke Grove and

Nightingale Crescent, the adjacent flats of the wicked, murderous, sluttish woman and the lovely Ms Jekyll. She wanted me, as I was to discover shortly after we had paused at the foot of Ms Jekyll's exquisite wrought-iron staircase, entwined at this time of year with geraniums and a small wall of sweet peas, to understand how close – how dangerously close the women had always been.

Ms Jekyll was sitting in the window of her flat. There was no doubt in my mind that it was she: Frances Crane had described her often enough – saying, with a laugh, that she was glad to be her friend but not her doctor (Dr Bassett fulfilled that function) as there always came a time in doctor-friend relationships when you have to refuse a request for something or other. And I wondered, remembering this, if, had Dr Crane been alive, she would have found something to be worried about in her friend's appearance today.

It's hard to define: just that, beautiful as I had expected her to be, Eliza Jekyll was even more perfect – almost impossibly perfect, with that tilt of the head and set of the neck that seem to go with beauty – and yet she seemed irredeemably sad. That old word melancholy came into my mind as I stood, half hidden by the chestnut tree at Tilda's side, and looked up at her. I remembered the photographs of Victorian madwomen incarcerated for 'eroticism', 'melancholy', even in one case 'intense vanity'. Ms Jekyll, as she sat staring at nothing in the window of her flat – she was on a sofa that had been pulled across the french windows, giving a further impression of someone barricaded in – looked as if she were badly in need of fresh air – or company.

Tilda put a foot on the first of the steps of the white iron stairs. 'Eliza!'

The face in the window turned; eyes sparkled; a charming smile appeared. 'Come out and see us!' Tilda pushed me a little forward. 'Someone here wants to meet you!'

Ms Jekyll rose, smiling and waving. (I was surprised to see that behind her, in the room, a pile of what looked like unwashed clothes and sheets threatened to topple from a table – and as if my glance in that direction had reminded her, she swung sharply round.)

I saw the back of her shoulders – we both did – convulsed with what must have been a sudden sobbing fit, or, worse, an attack of some kind that must surely need rapid medical attention. But with one hand the thick, interlined curtains were pulled to and the hunched trembling figure disappeared from our gaze. Like children at a conjuror's party, we stood, mouths open, for several seconds longer by the side of the chestnut tree.

'You know, I am very anxious for Miss Eliza,' Tilda said as we walked back slowly along the path of Robina's scruffy garden bordered by dark, unclipped shrubs. 'That woman is back – I know it. She will kill Eliza next!'

And Tilda wept, in the ragged long grass of her aunt's back garden. I thought, at first, of Jean Hastie and of summoning her down to deal with this. Jean, surely, had been here at the time of the murder. Jean alone had evidence of Dr Crane's last meeting with Eliza. Again, I realized I needed evidence myself if I were to risk calling her in her Scottish shooting party and asking her to come south and prevent further loss of life.

'I heard that woman Mrs Hyde in there the other day,' Tilda said, as if waiting for me to ask for proof. 'It was her voice. I know! She was shouting at poor Eliza!'

* * *

THE LAST EVENING

As it turned out, I didn't have to wait long to discover the truth of what Tilda said (Robina was sceptical about this, I have to say, and argued that if Mrs Hyde had indeed come back, the police of fifty countries would have been on her trail by now).

It was the following evening. Mara Kaletsky had just returned from a summer spent in gypsy caves in Hydra, and looked tanned and well; as if the whole nightmare of the killing in the gardens, and the hysteria over the rapist, had long ago gone from her mind. Robina had been kind enough to ask me round again; it was a fine evening, the gold sunlight as it poured into the long club room making even the dull of the old brass fender shine; and soon, when Monica Purves and her friend Carol Hill joined us, I saw that, for everyone, with the exception of Tilda, of course, the nightmare of the past was indeed over. I confess I had to wonder whether the girl's inflamed imagination hadn't been responsible for some of the unease I'd felt myself. It was true that Eliza Jekyll had turned away from us with a convulsive shudder; on the other hand it was possible that Tilda, who was quite an outspoken and annoying young woman, might have offended her at some dinner party to which she had been asked to come as a helper, and Eliza, with possible serious things on her mind, had turned away with a touch of intended melodrama, so as to warn us away from her window.

Whatever the truth was, an evening as pleasant as the one we were enjoying made one glad the rest of the Crescent was so empty; and a walk was soon suggested. Robina went to fetch the key to the back garden door and we all strolled out, only Tilda muttering an excuse and running upstairs to her room.

We hadn't gone far along the path when we saw the figure hurrying towards us. Monica Purves was the first to recognize the woman: Mrs Poole (for such it was) came sometimes to clean for her as she did, evidently, for Ms Jekyll. 'Oh, Miss Purves!' Mrs Poole seized hold of the stockbroker's sleeve, as if in need of something to help her keep her balance. 'There's been a terrible accident! That woman's come back and she's done away with Miss Jekyll, I know she has!'

* * *

JEAN HASTIE COMES SOUTH

I have to say at this point that I am now in possession of Jean Hastie's journals – and also the tape which Dr Frances Crane entrusted to her.

Jean may be a somewhat self-satisfied woman, but she left her family and house party as soon as she heard of the disappearance of Ms Eliza Jekyll and came south, stopping only at her firm's offices to retrieve the envelope sealed permanently unless there was a case of such a disappearance. She came straight to Robina's, after a bad night on a sleeper – and I must say she found us all as haggard as herself, sitting, as we had been all night, in the club room.

I won't go too far into the scene of chaos in Ms Jekyll's flat, once Monica had forced the french windows and we went in. Squalor needs no describing: what was worse were the evident signs of struggle, pointing almost inevitably to an attack – not dissimilar to the rapist's, as Carol Hill remarked with a grimace of strong distaste as she relived her own ordeal – and to the attacker having disposed of Eliza's body before making a getaway.

A door through the mirrored hall was open and there seemed little doubt – as dirty linen, spilled remains of junk food meals, etc., trailed from the (now equally filthy) apartment of Ms Jekyll into the run-down quarters of Mrs Hyde – of the identity of the murderer.

One mystery (for we had all learnt at the time of the Toller killing that the Hyde children had been placed in care) was irrefutable evidence of the recent presence of children. A potty had been used; and probably not all that long ago. Half-eaten fish fingers lay under a pile of broken Lego under the kitchen table. A small gym shoe, laces hopelessly knotted, had been kicked off by the door through to Ms Jekyll's Venetian-glass-panelled hallway.

'I don't know if they was back or not,' Mrs Poole said (having already given what evidence she possessed to the police she had returned to tell Jean what she had seen). 'I only know I heard a woman wailing like a banshee when I went round to give Miss Jekyll a hand with the flat. She'd not been in touch for – oh, it must have been near on eight weeks – but don't tell me that mess in there was her who done it.' Mrs Poole

shook her head firmly. 'She was got at by that Mrs Hyde
– wasn't she?'

'But you saw her?' Jean Hastie asked in that quiet, dry
way that reminds you of her training as a solicitor.

'Oh no, love. I just heard that terrible wailing sound.
Reminded me of a siren going off in the blitz, I can tell
you!'

After this unexpected piece of imagery, we all fell
silent.

'So you didn't see Mrs Hyde either?' Jean prompted
the woman.

'I sees the kids,' Mrs Poole said. 'They was playing
out by that dreadful old pianola-thing in the back garden, that the Council won't take, and I can't think why
she couldn't get rid of it herself. "Funny, how'd they
come to be here?" I remember thinking to myself. If I'd
just gone into Miss Jekyll's that day – if I hadn't just
waited one day more, but with my aunt in hospital –'

'It's not your fault,' Robina said, standing up so that
we could all feel released to go in the direction of hot
baths, breakfast, bed. 'The police will be searching for
Eliza Jekyll everywhere. They'll find her in the end.'

'They'll have to find Mrs Hyde first,' said Tilda,
appearing from her eyrie after a loud clattering down
the stairs.

* * *

After a day of rest, renewed speculation and
unanswered questions, Jean Hastie took the night train
back to Scotland, to be with her husband and young
family. She told me she had no desire to listen to the
tape; and that as I had been given the brief by Dr

Crane's solicitors to try and fathom the cause of the doctor's 'mystery illness' and death, she would prefer me to be its sole audience.

Mara Kaletsky invited me to come to her room at No. 19 Nightingale Crescent whenever I wanted, as home movies she had made of the opening of the Shade Gallery, etc. might be useful to me in my researches.

I have also put down as best I could my own impressions of the characters and setting of this odd tale; but if it hadn't been, once more, for Tilda, I would not now be in possession of a second, and vital, piece of oral evidence.

'The last time I saw Eliza,' Tilda said, 'on the day before we went round to call on her, she was sitting at a table by the window – she must have pulled the sofa across after that – and she was dictating a message into her answering-machine. I remember, because she was such a long time speaking, and I thought maybe she dictates addresses and phone numbers of somewhere she's going to.'

It was a weird feeling, calling the number of a person you know to have disappeared – and who, possibly, is also dead – but call I did.

Ms Eliza Jekyll's message, to whomsoever it may concern, is presented here, after Dr Crane's dictated jottings, in order to solve the mystery.

* * *

DR FRANCES CRANE'S NOTES AND MEMORABILIA

I was surprised to receive a letter from Eliza Jekyll on the day after her dinner party, May the eighth. We'd had a pleasant evening; it had been good to see an old friend in a less, I suppose one would have to say, exalted state than she had manifested on the infrequent and unsuccessful occasions of our meeting over the last year; and I must admit to a feeling of slight complacency on opening the envelope. Eliza was, in all probability, writing to thank *me* for coming to her dinner, and for openly resuming our friendship. That this was hardly the case was soon painfully evident.

I reproduce the letter in full, in the interests of medical science. And, I plainly confess, as a proof of my irremediable guilt in this grim and unsavoury business. My blindness and insensitivity as a member of the medical profession have led, in the main, to a state of affairs so appalling that no memory can encompass it without turning the corner from sanity into silence and madness.

This, as I know, is the path which is marked out for me. Yet my first reaction to Ms Jekyll's (hand-delivered) letter was that it was my correspondent who had gone mad.

Dear Frances,

I must ask you a favour. You will understand one day – and you will understand, too, the cause of a coolness between us – which came, I know from your disapproval of my way of life and general state of mind.

But for now – I really do beg you – just go round to my flat in Nightingale Crescent – Mrs Poole will let you in if you go as soon as you get this – and ask Mrs Poole to leave before you go to the little cabinet in the corner of my sitting room and open the door.

You can't miss it – the papier mâché cabinet with a scene on the door of a woman on a balcony, over-looking the sea. In the third drawer you will find a twist of white tissue paper. Take it out and wait for further developments.

This is a matter of life and death to me, Frances – please in the name of God do as I say.

Eliza

I had to move a patient to my partner Dr Bassett, all of which caused a good deal of inconvenience all round, but I went to the flat in Nightingale Crescent, half convinced, as I say, that I would have a duty to have my friend committed to a mental asylum by the end of the call.

Mrs Poole, as obviously arranged, let me in. But as far as a speedy exit from the flat went, this was not to be. I won't attempt to reproduce her speech, but the gist of what she said – and she was alarmed – considerably – I could see, amounted to a strong suspicion that violent and unpleasant scenes were taking place on the premises. There were tables overturned when she came in this morning, she said – and further signs of a struggle. That woman was back. That Mrs Hyde. And she was attacking her benefactor, who'd never in her life – and Mrs Poole knew this for a fact – done anything wrong. Miss Jekyll was hiding her somewhere here. And – this was the worst of it – when Mrs Poole had been coming back late from the pub with her husband and her sister-in-law last night, she'd heard such a sound coming out of this floor, such a sound as you couldn't for the life of you describe.

I asked Mrs Poole if she could nevertheless try. I was frightened, myself, I have to admit: and all the while we stood there talking I was keeping my eyes on this little cupboard in a corner of the room furthest from the window, with its dream-like, oddly disconcerting picture – like a Romantic opium scene, I suppose you might say – of a girl in a ball dress with bare shoulders sitting at a desk on a great sweeping balcony and beyond, rocks and the sea. The noise had at first been just a woman weeping, Mrs Poole said. But after that – her sister-in-law had said it was like a lost soul. And Mrs Poole, as if suddenly embarrassed by herself, proceeded to inform me she had to get to the shops before early closing and left the flat with all the bustle and sound of a denizen of this earth, lost soul or no.

I was both relieved and faintly alarmed by her going. But I went, steeling myself, to the squat little cabinet, knelt down, and opened the third drawer.

There, sure enough, was a twist of white tissue paper.

And there, on the back of a half-scrumpled envelope, was the name and phone number of London's most notorious doctor – a man who had deliberately allowed the deaths from overdoses of at least two world-famous rock stars; a man known to ask no questions while supplying lethal amounts of anything from amphetamine to crack, or heroin.

It wasn't hard, when I cautiously undid the twist of paper, to recognize the drug. We'd had enough patients in casualty at St Charles – young, nearly all of them, and supplied with the stuff no doubt at the clubs from which they were carried unconscious to an ambulance. So

Eliza Jekyll – I must say that my brain reeled at the thought of the composed and beautiful Eliza a secret addict of the most destructive and, as yet, largely unknown in its long-term effects, substance on the black market: by name, Ecstasy.

As I still knelt there, the doorbell rang. And, as I paused, wondering what these 'further developments' were going to turn out to be, it sounded again and again, with a desperation that seemed to come right through the entryphone system and into the room.

'Yes?' I said finally into the receiver – and beginning to be properly afraid, I have to admit, for the shuffling, whimpering sounds on the other side of the door were unmistakably those of the person – or thing – with its finger jammed down on the bell.

Of course, there was no answer. I didn't press the buzzer, but went to fling open the door of the flat.

The account of what followed must not be taken as a symptom of the increasing confusion and partial paralysis of the central nervous system which has succeeded the revelations of that brief quarter of an hour in Eliza Jekyll's flat. I was able to dictate notes immediately on return to my practice – with the door locked, it goes without saying – for fear that a colleague or patient might hear this tale of the – apparently – impossible.

Mrs Hyde stood at the door. The murderer of Jeremy Toller, subject of a worldwide police search, stood in front of me, hunched, whimpering, bedraggled, hand outstretched.

'Did you open the cabinet, Frances?' said the creature (for so, to my bitter shame, I confess I saw her). And, coming into the flat and pushing the door violently shut behind her – 'I was sent by Eliza. She sent me, Frances, to collect the – '

Here Mrs Hyde stopped, as she saw the twist of paper in my hands. Before I could pull away from her she was on me. Her teeth went into my neck – there was a vile smell clinging to her clothes, which were grey and streaked with grease as if she'd been sleeping rough in a railway station, as if, almost, the smell of sulphur she had on her had come up out of the ground to envelop her filthy clothes and cardboard shoes.

She was strong, that woman. Mrs Hyde had my arm in a half-Nelson – the hand that held the twist of paper soon relinquished its burden – and she leapt away from me, to press the contents flat down on the table.

On the round rosewood dining-table where only last night we'd all sat and discussed the coming Picasso exhibition and the Impressionist treasures from the Hermitage, Mrs Hyde sifted her drug and funnelled the paper to bring to nostrils gaping and greedy for the fix.

I should have known. And yet – how could it be? For, close to fainting, I saw the body of the most hated, the most vilified, the most hunted woman transform, translate itself, and, worse, for it should not be, to a form of beauty.

As the stooping shoulders straightened, the neck rose straight to bear a head – still dirty, true, but appearing now simply muddied by some rustic idyll or purposely for a glossy magazine sitting – that in its confidence of beauty and arrogance literally took my breath away. And the smile! Eliza's sweet, taunting smile, which I had seen her use to such good effect on Sir James Lister and others, was beamed steadily, and totally unself-consciously, on me.

'You see, Frances,' said this apparition, moving now to the hall and a line of fitted cupboards hidden in the mirrored walls. 'You have been treating me all along. But when you took me off the little helpers you first put me on so long ago, I was driven to find another to take their place. And Dr Ruby brought me back – well, almost from the dead!'

I couldn't find any words. It was as if – and this was perhaps the first onslaught of the famously rapid degenerative disease which has me in its grip – I had words stuck deep down in my throat and no muscle that would haul them up. I tried to ask Eliza, as she flitted into the bathroom and reappeared gleaming-faced and bright-eyed and as she wafted from the cupboard door in green raw silk suitable for the lovely May day outside, how she could fail to give herself up to the police: how she could live with the knowledge of the guilt of her crime.

But no words came.

And, with a backward, mocking glance at me, Eliza Jekyll walked out of the flat.

Yet the ultimate blame is mine.

I treated Mrs Hyde for anxiety. Three years ago I prescribed Anxian; and on a repeat prescription that demanded no vigilance from me.

In January this year Mrs Hyde called me. She said she was desperate. I saw evidence of neglect of her children and home. She admitted to violent impulses but would not divulge their exact nature. I prescribed Mrs Hyde's withdrawal from tranquillizers and advised a healthy diet and early nights.

It is only recently that the effects of withdrawal from these drugs has become known to the medical profession – and to the public at large. Heroin withdrawal symptoms are compared favourably with the effects.

By failing to keep in touch with the most recent discoveries on the nature of these pharmaceuticals and by continuing to allow Mrs Hyde to cash a repeat National Health prescription for them, I was surely condemning her to a state of dangerous disorder.

It is hardly surprising that, doubtless after reading one of those obnoxious newspaper articles, she went to the disreputable Dr Ruby.

Nothing can ever explain the personality change: its swiftness and its absoluteness. But we, as members of the medical profession, still have much to learn on the subject of personality disorders and their causes, both physiological and social.

I will not condemn Eliza to a lifetime in prison, and leave these notes for whomsoever shall find them – but only after my own death and/or the final disappearance of Ms Jekyll/Hyde.

* * *

MS ELIZA JEKYLL'S ANSAFONE MESSAGE

This is 229 46052. I'm afraid I can't answer your call at the moment. Please leave a message and speak after the bleep.

I have one last statement to make.
I am as I am: I was brought up to believe in happiness;

and my parents and schoolteachers gave me nothing but love and encouragement. I had no idea of the reality of life, of the pain and suffering which once was considered an integral part of it.

When the inevitable breakdown – for someone imbued with impossible dreams of happiness as I was – finally came, I was in no way capable of dealing with it.

My husband left me.

I became a slut. I struck my children.

My ex-husband's last visit to me was on the twelfth of February. He lives all round the world, and I live round these gardens, where I walk like a prisoner three times a day, rain or shine.

Sometimes I think of the man who comes to visit me as the rapist, and sometimes as the old rock star who owns the building and wants to tear it down and put it up again without me. Or the man who I went to see when I first took the drug and I put my hair up high and painted my nails and went out in high heels.

And he gave me the job. In the gallery.

But already the make-up wore off too soon, tired, tired.

And the meals lie round the kids' plates like a slug.

So on the nights when the birds first begin to mate, I went out in the frost and the room I'd rented and furnished on my new salary lay behind me like a Christmas decoration, and I killed the man as he came to lock up his precious family.

* * *

It would hardly be possible to make sense of a cursory message of this nature if it were not for Mara Kaletsky, who came to see me today and explained, after much beating about the bush, she 'had been keeping something from me all along'.

On the night of Eliza's disappearance, Mara says – before the final struggle overheard and reported by Grace Poole – she had gone round to the flat in Nightingale Crescent: first, as she points out with a trace of indignation, to demand why Eliza had done nothing to save her exhibition at the Shade Gallery; second, because she had 'a funny feeling that something was going on, and she couldn't say exactly what'. What she did see, in fact, was both surprising and intensely familiar to her, of course – for the features of Mrs Hyde, cut up and pasted down in so many of her collages, seemed, when the door of the elegant apartment was opened, to be fleetingly but unmistakably imprinted on the face of Eliza. It was like, Mara says, one of those images you get when you're half asleep – eidetic visions, she calls them (her next show will, she says, be composed of them, 'photographs from the sleeping brain') and there was an uncanny sense of unreality in Ms Jekyll's features – for a split second – as she opened the door and led Mara through into the mirrored hall. 'I've never experienced anything like it. Really – like hallucinating someone. And no wonder I thought so, because by the time we reached the window – it was a dark August day, remember, with the trees outside almost blocking the sky – and light came in on her, there was Mrs Hyde standing in front of me as plain as day.'

It was then that Mara decided to load her eternal video and shoot a roll of film. It's her response, one must suppose, to any situation – and perhaps Mara is no more than a presage of a world where the sole survivors are machines; where the images of people, imprinted like Fayoum portraits at the neck of ancient Egyptian tombs, speak in solitude and isolation to each other across time. Mara, it seems, has no way of answering human distress or communication other than to record it – yet Eliza Jekyll, doubled in her self and craving a true mirror image, clearly was as keen to speak into camera as any actress long starved of a part.

Mrs Hyde is speaking. It's eerie, to see the gardens framed by the french window behind her head: the gardens where the man lay dead in February. And it's shocking, somehow, to see her in Ms Jekyll's ornate quarters – though these, by now, are topsy-turvy with dirty clothes and broken plastic toy telephones, the detritus of a woman's life with children.

'I always had to tidy them away. If they offer you jobs they don't want to see a toy – a nappy – no.

'At first I pushed things under the chairs and into the cupboards. But then my big break came. I was able to rent this place – next to my own impossible flat – and I was offered a job almost straight away.'

'But first I should describe what my life has been.

'I was born and grew up in London. I went to art school in Oxford when I left school – it was there I met Jean Hastie. I'd have thought she'd have been more helpful to a woman in my circumstances. But, of course, she doesn't understand.

'I was just starting my first job, designing textiles for a big firm in the Midlands, when I met my husband. He was a journalist, doing pieces on working conditions, Trade Union legislation, that kind of thing.'

Here Mrs Hyde pauses, and Mara brings the camera right up to her. But she turns away, losing that face in the shadow from the rich, interlined curtains her new persona had put up to impress clients and keep out the undesirable elements of the world. All the same, the shudder of revulsion at her appearance remains: what is it about her except that she is clearly poor and ground down by life? What is it, other than the mesh of lines which seems, by catching her face so tight in its grasp, to have shrunk her head so that she appears to be both preserved, her head like a pygmy's head kept by a collector or hunter; and infinitely decayed, as if she could at any time disintegrate altogether, leaving on Mara's screen a pure, blank roomscape. Or is it just the reality of life's hard writing on her that makes her, seen through the eyes of guilt, so alien? Aren't there a vast number like her – persecuted by a hostile state? And facing hostility and fear from the public too?

Speculation of this kind is, however, countered by Mrs Hyde's succeeding statements. One can only wish, if the woman is found and brought to trial for the murder of Jeremy Toller, that she had not made this utterance: sympathy would otherwise surely have been forthcoming, for her position was, after all, not an enviable one, even if only too common.

'I may say', comes the voice of Mrs Hyde from the deep shadows by the curtain, 'that I was charmed by my husband – many were and still are – but I soon saw that there was no love there for either of us and knew I would soon be on my own.

'By this time I had two babies, eighteen months apart. The flat in Ladbroke Grove, on a fixed rent, was possible to find in those days – and it was the area where I had grown up – though it's changed now, of course, beyond recognition.

'I went on Social Security because there was no way at all that I could bring up these two young children and go out to a demanding job. I had no living relatives and only a few people who remembered me from the past. They, too, seemed sealed off in their worlds of trying to survive on little money and as single parents.

'I kept the kids clean and I cooked for them. They played in the communal gardens, but as the posh people moved in, their children threw stones at mine. Soon they were too frightened to go out there and we were all cooped up together in the flat.

'About this time I started having the dreams. Sometimes my husband came and saw me and sometimes I saw him in the dreams, and when he came we fucked occasionally, but it was hard because of the children. One night I dreamt I saw a tear the size of a big diamond lying on my hand and I felt a terrible grief inside, as if someone I knew very well – and loved – had died.

'When I woke, every morning after that, I knew some terrible change had come over me.

'Where I had been lithe and supple, with a dancer's legs and quick movements, I became slow and plodding as a sack of potatoes being dragged along the street. My neck shrank into my shoulders and my back began to develop a dowager's stoop, as if I was in turn dragging a great load of people through the world.

'But the waking moments were the worst. I would open my eyes – woken nearly always by a scream from one of the kids – and, for the first times at least, I had to do my best to repress a scream myself.

'There would be a hand lying on the pillow next to me.

'The hand was grey and wrinkled, and it was like a dead person's hand, limp and a darkish purple where the grey skin wasn't puckered by the join of finger and thumb. And – of course – it was my own ageing, defeated, accusing hand.

'I couldn't bear it. As the dreams went on, and I woke each time to the sight of this lame, dead piece of tissue and bone – which seemed more and more to stand for all of me, to be none of me but clearly what I had become – I began to cry and lose my temper with the children, and find pleasure only in plunging my hands in soap and suds so scalding hot that the little, half-broken Ascot over the sink would practically splutter itself out at the pressure of it.

'When I'd been hitting the kids so much I knew there might be a real battering in the night – an empty cot – a social worker called (and the nosy Mrs Poole was already round when I was shouting in a voice I didn't even know, and the kids were yelling like stuck pigs) and I went to Dr Crane at the Walmer Road practice.

'Well, the Anxian just made me cry the more. The world was grey, entirely grey. I threw out the pianola, which my husband had played once and which had some kind of a hurdy-gurdy colour to it, I suppose – and I watched it going grey in the little patch of balding grass that stands for a "patio" at this end of the communal gardens. The more I cried, the more the kids screamed. I tied them in their cots, but the social worker came again – and Dr Crane said they'd have to go.

'She was kind, Frances Crane. She didn't like people's kids being taken away. She put the drug under my skin, in the flesh just below that terrible hand. Nothing much happened at first – but then the dreams began to change and so did I.

'You can't imagine what it's like when your youth comes back – and beauty, and more – and the figure and the quick step to go with it. It only happened gradually at first, but I found out that if I took the pills my friend Marge gets from Dr Ruby from time to time it had some effect on the hormone drug and I could turn – just like that – into the person I had been. Yes, into me! Eliza! Where had I gone? Who had I been? But now – when I wanted, I was me!

'For I couldn't have it all the time. It wore off, faster and faster – but of course, as you know, Mara, I was at first Ms Eliza Jekyll most of the time and I went for the interview with Sir James Lister and I got the job running the Shade Gallery in Portobello Road.

'It was a long time since anyone had fancied me, and I couldn't think at first what Sir James was doing, making

113

those funny faces and rolling his eyes, when I sat opposite him at the interview. Then he bent down and gave me a little kick under the table, and I knew it was OK.

'I loved the power. Men would do anything for me. It was no problem getting this flat – from which of course I could go next door to my children – and the same landlord that had been round threatening "me" only the month before, was all over "me" as Ms Jekyll. But then I was paying a "commercial" rent, wasn't I, as Ms Eliza Jekyll?

'And I liked doing up the flat and giving dinner parties. The children went into a private nursery school. But one thing I desperately needed – and that was to buy the flat, the landlord was offering the freehold to those tenants who wanted them – and I wrote to Jean Hastie, asking her to do a conveyancing job for me.

'For if Mrs Hyde was the poor poor – that is, too poor to exist without State support – and even that dwindling (legislation changed for flat-renting so as sure as anything she'd be evicted from Ladbroke Grove) – then Eliza was the "rich poor", the individual encouraged to take out a hundred per cent mortgage: which "I" could, of course, with a job at the Shade and the hint from Sir James that I'd go on to run his design business in the South West.

'Jean was very stubborn; but I couldn't ask a London solicitor, who might know who I was. And, as my fear grew that my strange condition would become known, I realized I had to find and destroy those pictures of "me" that you had taken, Mara – of both of me, that is – for fear that the pieces of the collage might be put together

114

by some bright guy one day and I'd be rumbled. I went and hunted outside your studio, by the canal in Kensal Rise . . .

'As the fear grew, so did the rapidity with which the drug wore off. One day, coming back from Portobello Road where I had successfully been Eliza all day, I could feel myself change – and at the same time I could see Sir James Lister walking down Rudyard Crescent and coming towards me. Oh, brother! I said to myself. And – I have to tell you – the sensation of pure violence that poured through me was the most wonderful sensation I have ever had in my life. I was bow-legged by now, and my back was hunched up – and my hand, on the wheeled shopper I was pushing back with fine foods for the kids' supper was like the claw of some predator . . .

'And as he passed me I lunged at him and I ran him down. Well, I bumped into him hard, you might say . . .

'And all he saw was a poor, foul-smelling woman (for some reason these changes back to Mrs Hyde were always accompanied by a strong, unbearable smell, like escaping gas, and I always carried a raincoat with me, to cover the shrinking body and the odour of putre-faction).

' "Hey there!" he shouted.

'But he didn't think it worth his while to go after me. This man who had tried to fondle my breasts only an hour before! Who had invited me to a Valentine's Day lunch at the Pomme d'Amour restaurant in Holland Park Avenue!

'But that was a date, of course, that I was in no position to take up . . .'

On the night of the twelfth of February – just a few days after this – I gave my dinner party. I was worried about you finding out the truth, Mara, because you had been behind me in the street when I ran at Sir James . . . but you didn't seem to think anything strange was going on whatsoever.

'I knew better. My dreams had come back again, and the night before I'd heard the birds getting ready for an almighty burst for spring.

'I was Mrs Hyde . . . unexpectedly and terrifyingly . . . more and more often; and that night I knew I was poised, like a china cup that might fall from a shelf at the slightest tremble of the earth, and go into a million different pieces.'

'The landlord had been round to Ladbroke Grove and had informed me that I must pay a large sum towards the renovation of the 'common parts' of the building. I told him I wouldn't; and he told me there were a good many ways of getting me out.

'That was the day before. On the evening of the dinner, my husband – or ex-husband as he is – came to "see the kids". I wanted him out. He'd spoil my play for the big job with Sir James – and I was prepared to go all the way for it, I can tell you. Turning up just when he knows it'll wreck the chance of a new life for me – the no-maintenance fucking bastard.'

Mrs Hyde paused again. Then she stepped out from the folds of the curtain; and, as Mara records, something like the beginning of a return transformation must have been taking place, for she looked taller, handsome, almost.

'I got him out in the end,' says this new apparition. 'But it tired me, I can tell you, Mara. By the time the guests – and the food and the waiter – came, I was a wreck.

'Somehow I got through the dinner. All the talk of the rapist was getting on my nerves – especially as "I" in my persona as Mrs Hyde (who was unable to prevent myself from running naked in her terrible anger in the gale-lashed gardens) was actually a heroine now, as far as you, and most of the more radical women in the neighbourhood, were concerned.

'When everyone had gone I went out into the gardens to get some air. I could hardly believe what I had heard from Sir James – it had been couched, of course, in evasive language – but it seemed he was getting out of England altogether and setting up business in California – and the concomitant suggestion that both the Shade Gallery and his textile business would close down had been left hanging in the air between us. I walked a little; came back into the flat, and I must have fallen asleep. I woke at some dead hour of the early morning. And there . . . hanging by my side . . . like a dead rodent . . . like something that has been dragged in and left to die . . . was the hand of Mrs Hyde.

'For the first time, I had changed as I slept: the Yuppie who took a quick nap after a successful dinner party had woken the avenging slattern, practically a witch in the locality by now, hated and despised by the respectable inhabitants of these leafy crescents and squares.

'I went out into a night that had the false dawn of a London night hanging above it like a cloud from a crematorium. The birds began to strike up. Valentine's

Day . . . two hearts indeed, I thought, as I saw a man walk down towards me on the path . . . two hearts, my sweetheart, beating as one in the dawn of spring.

'The rapist walked there, Mara, with the face of my husband and the landlord's long, straight legs, and the slight pot belly of Sir James.

'The rapist loomed and leered at me.

'With the parrot head umbrella Ms Jekyll carries wherever she goes I walked towards that Valentine man; and I smiled at him as if it were the most normal thing in the world to be out walking in the middle of the night, in the gardens.

'He looked worried as he passed me. I dimly saw there was a dog at his heels, a little white thing I'd grown to hate, as it bit the kids when they went out.

'He looked surprised – that was all. For, after going past him, I nipped as suddenly as the time I felt the change come on me in the gallery when I ran to heave – against my will and with all the will in the world – a brick through the window of the place – I nipped sideways and behind him and hooked him round the collarbone with that parrot on a stick with nylon wings.

'Thank God – I could change quickly back to Eliza Jekyll that night. And next day I had to stand by and watch them take Mrs Hyde's children into care.'

The film ends suddenly here. There's a run of white tape; and then a black and white fuzzy scene, as if a child was doodling with a pencil on a dirty piece of paper.

'She begged me not to follow her,' Mara says. 'And I didn't. Don't tell me I was wrong.'

I said I wasn't telling her anything.

'I gave her all the money I had,' Mara says. 'She promised to hide in the cellar. And then she climbed up from the basement and hid under the dug-up street until I gave her the all-clear.'

There was a silence.

'Where are the children?' I asked. 'And why did they come out of care?'

'Jean Hastie applied to foster them – in Scotland,' Mara replies, as if it had been dumb of me not to see that there was kindness in the Scottish lawyer, all along. 'Jean told Eliza that if there was trouble, she'd bring the children up. She guessed some of this, I think.'

Or she listened to Dr Crane's notes, I thought to myself. And, before I could imagine Mrs Hyde's children's transformation into bairns in the hands of Jean Hastie and her husband, Mara had added quietly that, although Mrs Hyde, still sought internationally for the murder of businessman and local magistrate Jeremy Toller, had briefly been sighted on a cross-channel ferry from Weymouth to Cherbourg, there had apparently been no sign of her whatsoever on board when the French gendarmerie swarmed on to the boat.

'Mrs Hyde came up into Ladbroke Grove,' says Mara. 'But by the time she was in France – well, she must have been Eliza Jekyll again.'

'Or', I couldn't help remarking, 'for all – as Jean Hastie would say – that the woman had killed and must answer for the crime, perhaps she has at last been able to find herself.'

AFTERWORD BY JEAN HASTIE

Fife, Christmas '88

It was today that I posted the manuscript of my work on Original Sin to the publishers in London and a copy to my agent in Edinburgh.

Despite my conviction, earlier in the year, that my research on Original Sin in the Garden of Eden, showing a choice for Christians up until the fourth century and the coming of St Augustine between salvation and damnation, was conclusive evidence of an innate sense of moral responsibility in each individual, I have to say here that I am no longer certain on this – all-important – point.

The case of Eliza Jekyll has caused a considerable rift in both Christian and atheist feminist thinking.

For, while it is incontestably true that the stress and discrimination suffered by a single mother in an environment growing daily more hostile in both financial and psychological terms can cause defensive violence as well as misery and frustration, it is also true that Eliza has proved to have been the harbourer of sentiments and impulses which can only be described as evil. Scribbled notes found by the bed of Mrs Hyde, in the final clear-out of her flat, attempt to give some substance to the 'bad dreams' the poor woman suffered in her phase of acute Anxian withdrawal.

That these were not dreams but murderous intentions is borne out by the knife she describes as hiding under the floorboards of the kitchen – and which was found there, under cork tiling disintegrating to the touch.

The knife was brandished at the rapist – as Mrs Hyde went out to get him that night in February, but naked, under the see-through white plastic mac.

He got away – that time. The police caught him in the end. But Mrs Hyde – will they ever catch her?

I keep hidden from her children, who stay with me here and breathe the purer air of Scotland, any news stories or headlines that crop up in the search for their mother. And I'll make sure they don't find the other side of this tragic victim of our new Victorian values: the word, scrawled across the pad under a list of household essentials –

> Ajax
> fishfingers
> ketchup
> Mother's Pride

> KILL